THE HUNGER PAINS

THE HUNGER PAINS is a work of fiction. Names, characters, places, poisons, and incidents are products of the author's imagination or used fictitiously. Any resemblance to actual events, locales, or persons, living or dead, is entirely coincidental.

Published by JFP Trust
2016 First Print Edition

ISBN: 978 0 9945756 3 0

Printed in the United States of America.

www.chelseafieldauthor.com

For my greyhound, Asha.

The least doglike dog I know.

1

NO WAY WAS I GOING to let them win. I sucked in a deep breath and fought the denim fabric straining against my hips. With white-knuckled fingers and the power of positive thinking, I managed to do up the top button. Aha!

I straightened to survey myself in the mirror and got a glimpse of short copper-brown hair, blue eyes, and an oxygen-starved face before the aforementioned button launched itself free of my jeans and rolled under the bed. My housemate's cat, Meow, who had been fast asleep on my pillow, dived after it like it was a cockroach. Her favorite prey.

Jeans: one. Izzy: zero. I stripped them off and left them discarded on the floor in disgust. My client, Earnest, sat in front of his computer all day eating snack food, which meant I sat around all day eating the same. His metabolism allowed him to get away with it. Mine, not so much. Three months in, that button was a message. A message I didn't have time for right now. I was running late, and while Earnest Dunst was in some ways the most easygoing client in the world, he didn't deal well with a disrupted routine.

My phone buzzed with an alert.

That outfit is perfect. You look wonderful. Now hurry up and leave.

I looked down at myself and snorted. I was wearing a pair of hipster briefs that had once been red, a white sports bra, and gray socks that had a hole in each heel. Not the best outfit for fighting my way through Los Angeles's morning traffic.

After I'd arrived late a couple of times, Earnest, in his infinite geekiness, had designed a phone app to help me be on time. It sent motivational text messages until my phone's GPS proved I'd left the house. The texts were selected by some algorithm that meant I never had the same sequence twice. Almost all of them made me laugh. None of them made me on time.

I snatched a pair of black sweats off the floor. They were more presentable than most, with a slim fit that could pass for real pants if no one looked too closely. They also had an elastic waistband. And were covered in Meow's hair. I threw my legs into them, pulled on a loose-fitting top to cover my extra pounds and the telltale drawstrings, then grabbed my phone, bag, and keys.

My phone told me I should've left four minutes ago. Not long by most people's standards, but time stretches differently for anxious, routine-reliant agoraphobics. Still, I couldn't resist reaching under the bed for the button and sending it spinning across the room for Meow.

She pounced, and my phone buzzed.

Your teeth are like a flock of newly shorn sheep (that's a Bible verse I read once. I think it's supposed to be a compliment). The point is you can skip brushing them this morning.

I ran out to the kitchen and started transferring the white-chocolate-and-raspberry muffins from the cooling rack into a container. My phone rang, and I answered without looking at the number. "Hello?"

"Izzy, I'm glad you picked up." It was Etta, my septuagenarian neighbor who far surpassed me in both style and sexual conquests. Not that either was hard to do. "You like me, right?"

"Uh, yes. Of course." No one would call Etta insecure. Something was up.

"And you owe me since you had that last adventure without me."

"You mean the adventure where I got shot?" My weight gain had started when I was forced into a sedentary routine after a bullet ripped through my leg. No one had forced me to eat all the cookies though.

"That's the one."

"What do you want?"

"I need your help moving a body."

Oh boy. I so did not have time for this. I stuffed the last muffin in the container and unlocked the deadbolt and chain on the front door. A small layer of safety I'd added to the apartment after an unwanted guest broke in. Twice. "Where are you?"

"At the bottom of the stairs."

Our 1960s concrete box of a three-story apartment building in Palms, Los Angeles, shared the external set of stairs I was standing on. So I could've leaned over the railing and looked, but I wasn't quite ready to face it.

Instead, I locked the door behind me. Christmas was just nine days away, and my housemate, Oliver, had eschewed the traditional wreath and stuck up a poster. It said *Merry Chrismyass* and featured a picture of Santa bending over to bare his second set of rosy cheeks.

I sniggered as I did every time I saw it, then asked Etta the question I'd been avoiding. "Is this body dead or alive?"

"Alive."

The giant corkscrew in my shoulders unwound a few rotations. "I'll be right there." I disconnected and glanced at the last message from Earnest.

Don't mind me. I don't need any sustenance this morning because I'm a robot.

Shaking my head, I hurled myself down the two flights of steps as fast as I could manage and found Etta leaning on the banister like she was posing for a fashion shoot. Her soft white hair was down today, falling around her face in loose curls, and her oversized white silk shirt echoed the effect. Charcoal wool leggings, nude leather ankle boots, and a string of pearls completed the outfit. She might have looked like a benevolent angel but for her blue eyes and bony figure that were both a touch too sharp.

That and the cigarette dangling from her fingers.

At her feet, a large, skinny dog was stretched out flat on its side on the sidewalk. He was sleek black except for a stripe on his nose, three white paws, and a smudge of gray on his muzzle.

"Is that a greyhound?" I asked.

"Yes. Izzy, meet Dudley. My new gentleman companion. He's an early Christmas present to myself."

With Christmas right around the corner, reminders of the season were everywhere. From billboards, radio, and TV ads shouting about this year's attractions, to the explosion of twinkle lights, ice-skating rinks, and fat men in red suits that had taken over the city. Of course, in California the skating rinks were artificially frozen, and any snow was made of styrofoam. Even so, the weather was turning cold by LA standards, and it would be my first wintry Christmas.

Back home in Adelaide, Australia, the holiday was a shorts and flip-flops affair in 104 degrees. We still ate roast turkey; we just washed it down with ice cream.

Dudley barely reacted to my breakneck arrival. He stared up at me with big brown eyes and flopped his tail once against the concrete.

"Is Dudley okay?"

Etta nudged him with her boot. "He's fine. It's only that he's never seen stairs before and is feeling a little overwhelmed."

I squatted down to pet him. He sniffed me inquisitively and gave another lazy tail wag. "How can I help?"

"I was hoping you could carry him. I'll teach him how to use the stairs soon, but he's never seen anything besides his cage and a racetrack, so today I want to get him inside and let him relax."

I considered Dudley, who had yet to lift his head from its hard pillow. "He looks pretty relaxed to me." Then I noticed again how large he was. About the size of a full-grown deer. And a similar shape, come to think of it. "Wait. You want me to *carry* him up the stairs? How much does he weigh?"

"Eighty pounds."

Well. It was a lot, but it was also a lot less than me. I sent a quick text to Earnest saying I was going to be late and looked again at Dudley. I'd just been thinking how I needed to burn some excess calories. Why not start now with some strength exercises?

"Can you get him to stand up?" Weight loss or not, there was no way I could peel eighty pounds off the concrete.

Etta patted her leg. One of Dudley's ears pricked forward, but nothing else moved. "Come on, you can do it." She took a few steps backward, and he heaved himself to his feet. "Good boy!"

Revising the manual handling procedures I'd learned to move large trays of bakery products in my former life, I put my arms around Dudley's chest and hind legs, braced my back, and stood up. With his body tucked against mine, I told myself it wasn't that bad and started up the stairs.

Dudley stayed as motionless as a statue, which was a great help, but by the time I reached the first landing, my legs were shaking. I might've put him down for a rest if I hadn't been unsure whether I'd be able to pick him up again. I leaned against the rail for a second to catch my breath.

Etta looked at my trembling limbs. "You know, if you'd stayed together with Connor, he would've carried Dudley up like it was nothing."

She wasn't ready to forgive me for "breaking up" with Connor. My former client. He was the kind of man who made a woman hot and bothered in both senses of the words, and our relationship had been fake from day one, but Etta didn't know that. In fact, it was part of my job to ensure she never knew that. The joys of working undercover.

"That's very helpful, thanks." I panted.

"Just saying."

"Speaking of how heavy Dudley is, isn't he rather large for your small apartment?"

"Nope. Greyhounds make great apartment dogs."

"Don't they, uh, like to run?" Not that Dudley had shown any sign of it. I needed to run, though, if I didn't want Earnest to have a meltdown. My phone buzzed in agreement. I lurched away from the railing and started up the last set of steps.

"Sure, for a few minutes a day. The rest of the time they sleep or laze around. They call them forty-five-mile-per-hour couch potatoes."

Dudley was one heavy potato. But I couldn't judge. I reached the second landing and plonked him down as gently as I could manage. My back twinged despite the manual handling procedures, so I took a moment to straighten up. Dudley used the opportunity to lick my nose. Then, invigorated from his nap on the concrete, he trotted off to explore the landing, tail waving like a banner of happiness.

I felt a smile play on my lips. "Welcome home, Dudley." Then I fished my phone out of my pocket and scanned the latest text.

If you really hate being late, how come you're so good at it?

I ARRIVED IN UNIVERSITY PARK eleven minutes behind schedule. I was expecting Earnest to be upset with me, seeing as he hadn't replied to my text. I wasn't expecting him to be so upset that he wouldn't answer the door.

Or perhaps he was just engrossed in a computer game. Once, he'd been so focused that I'd managed to rearrange the whole living room behind him into a mirror image of its normal self. The look on his face when he got up for the bathroom a few hours later and saw me sipping a cup of tea on the rotated couch was worth every strained muscle.

Now I rummaged through my bag for the spare key he'd given me. The key I'd never had to use in the two and a half months I'd been his Shade—or his undercover poison taster for those not familiar with the term.

A siren wailed nearby, reminding me that while University Park was one of the better neighborhoods in Central LA, it had double the crime per capita of my own chosen suburb of Palms. Of course, the poisoning attempts I was paid to protect Earnest from didn't show up in crime statistics.

I located the key at last. Now I was thirteen minutes late.

The tiny one-bedroom apartment was too cramped for a Christmas tree, so the place was a tinsel-free zone. "Earnest?"

No answer. Not that it mattered. I knew exactly where I'd find him. "I'm sorry I'm late. My neighbor got this new dog and—"

He wasn't in front of his computer.

I pushed away a prickle of foreboding. He was probably on the toilet.

Figuring he wouldn't want me to look for him in there, I went into the kitchen to set about getting breakfast ready. The cooking area was about the size of a postage stamp, with chipped cupboards painted lavender by a previous tenant and just enough counter space for a kettle and a cockroach or two. It was adequate for Earnest's needs. Two eggs, sunny-side up on toast, and a bowl of Froot Loops. The same breakfast he had every morning.

It's not that he was obsessive-compulsive exactly. Agoraphobia is an anxiety disorder, and it helped him feel more safe and in control if everything was familiar and within the boundaries of a routine. Staying inside his home achieved the same thing: familiar boundaries. An environment he could control.

Since it meant my job as his Shade consisted of hanging around his place and feeding him every now and then,

I was happy to oblige. I was starting to think the Taste Society paid me too much. A hundred grand a year, and here we were, ten weeks in without a single poisoning attempt. Even better, Earnest only ever invited two other people over, so I hardly had to maintain my girlfriend cover story.

It made paying off my crippling debt to the loan shark seem doable—not like the life sentence I'd once thought it was.

Best client ever.

I hummed to myself as I slid the eggs onto the toast and added salt and pepper. Then I tasted it for poison. In the mild flavors of the dish, most harmful substances would be simple to detect, but I forced myself to take my time, to be extra careful. On this job, a moment of inattentiveness could cost my client his life. A fact that had been drilled into me during training. And with Earnest's uneventful, repetitive routine, it would be all too easy to relax.

The food was clear, of course. Transferring the plate to the crook of my arm to make room on the teeny countertop, I poured Froot Loops and milk into a bowl and tasted those as well. The artificial flavors and sugary sweetness were harder to discern through, but I'd memorized the distinct profile of each poison by tasting them firsthand so I knew what to look for. Also clear.

"Breakfast is ready when you are!"

Still no answer. Maybe he had gastrointestinal issues. I would have if I'd eaten two bags of Cheetos Bolitas yesterday.

More likely he was playing some kind of game on his phone and was lost in that special place men seem to find when they take a dump.

I carried the plates over to the dining table and sat down, listening to the crackle of the Froot Loops, and waited. Ironic, given how much I'd rushed to get here. My mind replayed the button rolling across the floor and suggested I do some sit-ups while I waited. My sore back suggested otherwise.

I wondered how Dudley was finding his new apartment. If his experience up until now had been limited to his cage and the racetrack, he'd have never seen carpet, or a couch, or a mirror. Or heard a vacuum cleaner run or a toilet flush. Or tasted eggs on toast. Or bacon. No wonder the stairs had been overwhelming. I would find all of life overwhelming without bacon.

As a result, I have a lot of respect for Jews and Muslims.

Six minutes later, with Earnest's eggs cold and Froot Loops soggy, I decided special place or not, I was going to interrupt. I went into his bedroom, the door already open, and knocked on the en-suite door.

No answer.

"Come on, I said I was sorry."

No answer.

"I'm coming in unless you say something."

No answer.

He was starting to worry me now. I eased the door open slowly, giving him one last chance to look up from his phone's screen and yell out. Nothing.

The bathroom was empty. A flutter of fear passed through my stomach. How had I managed to misplace my agoraphobic client?

Praying I wouldn't find him cold and motionless on the floor somewhere because I'd been so late he'd eaten without me, I searched the rest of the apartment. It didn't take long, and it was as empty as the bathroom.

Okay. Don't panic. That was good, right? If he'd been poisoned, he would be here. So maybe he was out with one of his safe people. He did leave the house on very rare occasions in the presence of his mother or his best friend Jay Massey. Maybe he forgot to tell me. Unlikely, given he would've been worrying about it, but possible. Or maybe they'd surprised him with a last-minute outing. Then in his anxiety he might not have remembered to let me know. That was plausible.

I dialed his number, half expecting to hear his *Star Wars* "Imperial March" ringtone somewhere nearby. The apartment was silent, though, and his phone went straight to voice mail. Dead battery? It wasn't like Earnest to neglect to charge any of his technological gadgets. He treated them with the same love and tenderness as Etta had for her Glock.

Fortunately, I'd accumulated both of his safe people's phone numbers over the months of playing the part of his girlfriend. I dialed his mom first. "Hey, Mrs. Dunst. It's Izzy here."

"Oh hello, darling girl. How are you?"

"I'm good. I was just wondering if you know where Earnest might be?"

"He's not at home? Have you tried Jay?"

"Not yet. I'll call him now."

I called Jay.

"What do you want?" he asked, doing a decent impression of Aunt Alice the time I'd told her she looked nice (I was six and wanted to try on her lipstick). Jay had been suspicious of me from day one, unconvinced I was interested in Earnest for anything but his money. Technically, I guess I was with Earnest for the money, but beneath the geeky, agoraphobic exterior, he was sweet and funny and brave, and I liked him a lot. Even more than Aunt Alice's lipstick, which I never did get to try on.

"I was wondering if Earnest is with you? He's not at—"

"Nope, he's not with me."

"Right, thanks anyway."

I slumped down by the unsalvageable breakfast and failed to come up with any positive scenarios to fling at the fear that was tightening my innards. Earnest was missing. Without either of his safe people. Without either of his safe people even knowing where.

I could think of only two options. One, he'd relapsed. He'd been clean for fifteen months and mostly clean for three years, but he'd told me once an addict, always an addict, and heroin was the one thing that might overcome his anxiety enough to leave the house unaccompanied. Two, he'd been taken against his will. Neither were good options.

Mrs. Dunst called me back. "Did Jay know where he was?"

"No. I've been trying to work out what to do."

"Sweet cartwheeling weasels. He must have fallen off the wagon again." She took a big breath and let it out a little shakily. "It's not the first time, but I always hope it's the last, you know? What are you doing, darling? Can you help me look?"

For a moment I was too distracted by the image of weasels doing cartwheels to answer. Considering how cute they were, I snapped out of it pretty fast. "Of course. But shouldn't we call the authorities? What if he whistle-blew the wrong group of people?"

Earnest was loaded enough that he could've spent the rest of his life gaming, but after getting clean, like his sci-fi heroes, he wanted to fight evil and do good.

Sadly, the real life version had fewer spaceships.

He started the website BusiLeaks, which was pretty much the equivalent of WikiLeaks for corporate America: a trusted source of leaked information on misconduct and cover-ups by US companies. It meant he pissed off a lot of powerful people, which is why he hired me.

In spite of the stories spun by public relations, the cut-throat climb to fame and fortune is more like *The Hunger Games* than the standards of behavior they teach you in kindergarten. If you can't outmaneuver the competition, you can always poison them and tell the world it was a tragic drug overdose.

"Oh dear. You've let him fill your head with his paranoia," Mrs. Dunst said. "Part of his anxiety disorder, the poor dear thing, is that he thinks everyone's out to get him. The only people who read that website are conspiracy nuts."

The conspiracy nuts weren't so far off. In addition to the well-concealed murders, around a third of those news stories about celebrities ruining their careers while under the influence are in reality carefully planned sabotage. The authorities help cover it up since no one wants to popularize poisoning among the masses.

Besides, five million hits on Earnest's last post demonstrated how well respected BusiLeaks was, but I held my tongue. For some reason, he'd never bothered to set his mother straight, perhaps so she wouldn't realize how dangerous it had the potential to be. How dangerous it might be proving itself to be, right at this moment.

I didn't want to think about gentle, anxious Earnest in cruel hands. He'd been unsettled enough by that double yolker in his breakfast a few weeks back.

I squared my shoulders. I'd give us two hours. If we hadn't found him by then, I was calling in for reinforcements. My employer, the Taste Society, had all sorts of systems in place for protecting their clients. Most of them were above my clearance level, but they were all discreet and effective.

First though, I needed to make sure he was really missing.

I pulled the phone closer. "Where should I search?"

WORRY FOR EARNEST still gnawed at my gut, but having a plan of action helped me dull its sharp teeth.

I walked up to the first location Mrs. Dunst had assigned to me. Naively, my attention was focused on finding Earnest rather than the fact I was entering a drug den.

It was a small blue-rendered home in the middle of an overgrown junkyard lot. I stepped over a severed doll's head, the faded eyes staring up at me as I passed. A mound of tires leaned ominously over the path, and I hurried past those too. Raising my hand to knock, I realized there was nothing to knock on. Only a screen door stood between me and the interior, and the screen had come loose and hung halfway down the frame. No Christmas decorations here either.

"Hello?" I called.

A shuffling came from within, sounding more like a huge wounded lizard dragging itself along the ground than a person. I stepped back, unable to see more than a few yards inside the gloomy interior thanks to the covered windows.

Blinds were a rarity, but the tenants had improvised. The nearest one had a mattress leaning against it.

Something emerged from the darkness. A human, not a lizard, though the knot of hair on their head could be mistaken for a dead one. I wasn't sure if they were male or female from the gaunt face and skeletal frame. The source of the shuffling noise was a pair of novelty-sized gorilla slippers, complete with human-looking toes poking through the matted fur.

"Whaddya want?" The voice was too gravelly to shed any light on their sex.

"Um. I'm trying to find Earnest." I held up the photo Mrs. Dunst had told me to bring. It was a six-by-four-inch print I'd nicked from one of Earnest's photo frames because she'd warned me to leave all my valuables in the car. Then again, the most valuable thing I possessed was the car—a twelve-years-young silver Corvette—and it wasn't mine. It was a perk of the job. "Have you seen him?"

The vacant gaze didn't even flicker toward the photo. "Nope."

"Are you sure? It's important."

The person grunted and shuffled back into the gloom.

I guessed that was a no.

I slid onto the cool leather driver's seat, unsure whether to be relieved or not. It was my first glimpse into the bleak horror of what Earnest had escaped from. Would it be better or worse to find him here, out of his mind on heroin?

What if we couldn't find him at all? The gnawing worry sharpened its teeth. Was it foolish not to call in the Taste Society right away? But second-guessing myself wasn't helping anyone. I'd stick with the plan.

Hoping the lizard person wasn't indicative of the type of help I was going to get for the rest of my search, I drove to the next address. This one looked more hopeful. The building and yard were better maintained, and heavy metal music blasted from the windows, promising someone was home. It even had a life-size plastic snowman on the lawn, although he seemed to be holding a bong in his twiggy hand.

A muscular young man answered my knock. I could tell the muscular thing because he'd forgotten his shirt. He noticed my eyes on his chest and smirked.

I tried to use it to my advantage. "Hi. I'm Izzy. Isobel Avery, I mean. Ernie's girlfriend." I pitched my voice higher than normal and made it sound like a question.

This got a grunt.

I twirled my finger through my hair and angled another glance at his chest, aiming for hesitant attraction. "Um. He didn't come home last night, and I was wondering if you'd seen him?"

The guy looked at my chest too.

I stuck the picture of Earnest in front of it and was gratified when he gave it his attention. "Nah. Haven't seen him." His eyes met mine. "But I can show you a good time while he's away, baby."

"Uh, thanks, but I need to find him."

He bounced his pectoral muscles. "I'll make you forget he ever existed."

I backed away, resisting the urge to run. "Maybe later." No point alienating the guy. At this rate, he might be my most helpful lead. Plus I was kind of impressed by his muscular control.

I retreated back to my car and traveled to two different locations with similar results. Which meant Earnest hadn't bought heroin from any of his old haunts or no one was talking. Then again, given the track marks in their arms and their unfocused expressions, they might have had a deep and meaningful conversation with him five minutes before and forgotten all about it. Kind of like old Mr. Gileppi who used to come to the bakery I'd worked at every Tuesday and tell me about the birth of his new granddaughter. Ten weeks in, I figured he either had a lot of children who'd decided to reproduce at the same time or his memory wasn't quite right.

It was painful to imagine Earnest being one of the addicts I'd met today. He was highly intelligent and passionate about helping others. And about gaming. And Cheetos Bolitas. These people had no passion, no personality, no life or laughter. It had all been swallowed by addiction. I was as scared about finding him as not.

I parked my Corvette outside my second-to-last stop before reconvening with Mrs. Dunst and calling my Taste Society handler. It was an old clapboard building in Exposition Park, marked for demolition. The warped timber door was rough and splintery under my hand as I pushed it aside. With the windows boarded up and the electricity switched off long ago, the interior was even more gloomy than the lizard person's house. I paused to switch on my phone's flashlight before stepping inside.

Hair stood on the back of my neck. Not creepy at all. A thick layer of dust coated everything except for a well-used trail of footprints leading into another room. I followed it, trying not to notice the smaller trails of rat footprints that skittered everywhere or the cobwebs coating the corners. It smelled of stale garbage and dirt.

I eased through the doorway, still following the footprints, and stopped dead.

No.

Rats scurried away from the light to reveal a bundle of clothing. Clothing that looked eerily familiar after seeing the same outfit every day for the past few months.

Please no.

I took a step closer. The rats had nibbled on his face, but it was unmistakably Earnest.

Dear, sweet, geeky Earnest. Best client ever.

There was no need to check for a pulse.

2

I FOUND MYSELF STUMBLING into the daylight. My eyes watered as they adjusted to the brightness, and I vomited my muffin onto some bluegrass weeds.

My eyes were still watering as I straightened up, and I realized I was crying. Sobbing noisily, in fact.

It can't be true. Earnest can't be dead. He was only twenty-nine years old. The same as me. I wanted to be lying on his couch, laughing at him while he made up a song to help me remember the "vital takeaways" of the 1950s movie, *Forbidden Planet.* I wanted to see his hazel gaze widen in abject horror when I admitted to not knowing how to use an Xbox One controller, then light up when I asked him to show me. I pinched myself like it might make the nightmare go away.

It didn't.

Long minutes passed before I could pull myself together enough to call my Taste Society handler.

"Identify yourself," Jim answered.

My relationship with Jim hadn't improved since our first phone call when I'd tried to win him over with my sparkling personality. Jim didn't like sparkles. I didn't like his professional indifference. So I'd made a habit of annoying him just to get a reaction.

Now, though, I recited the ID number without any commentary. Too upset to be irksome. "Shade 22703. I'm calling to report the death of my client."

"Natural or suspicious?"

"I don't know."

"Well, is there poison involved?"

"I don't know."

"Are you sure he's dead?"

The memory of his sightless hazel eyes flashed before me. "Yes."

Jim grunted. "Right. That's one thing at least. I'll send the nearest investigator to your GPS coordinates. Sit tight."

The acrid smell of puke made my stomach even more sour, so I retreated to my Corvette. How could this happen? Except for the calculated risk of his BusiLeaks site, Earnest did everything he could to stay safe. Triple-checked his facts before publishing anything. Hired a Shade. Never left his apartment. Was careful who he invited inside. That should be enough.

Unless he was sick of being housebound and took heroin to overcome his anxieties. Could he have done it to himself?

It looked that way, but then so did most high-profile murders.

If Earnest was murdered, had his life ended here, or was it only a dumping ground? I thought back to the footprints. There was an almost dust-free path in the middle where something might have been dragged, but it could also be the result of extra foot traffic as I'd originally assumed. I'd know more if I went in and looked, but I would leave that to the investigator.

A small voice told me I was focusing on the mechanics of the case to avoid the raw grief inside me. I told the small voice that it seemed as good a strategy as any.

A knock on the driver's window interrupted this enlightening conversation with myself before it could deteriorate into name-calling. I saw cool gray eyes and a familiar mouth pulled in a familiar hard line. All the moisture in *my* mouth evaporated, and I got out of the car.

"You again," Connor Stiles said.

I was a little offended at that greeting from my first-ever client and former investigating partner (okay, partner was a bit of a stretch; he led, I trailed after him asking mostly pointless questions). I hadn't seen him in three months, but I'd dreamed about him much more recently.

Refusing to let my disappointment show, I willed some saliva to emerge so I could free my tongue from the roof of my mouth. "Merry Christmas to you too." He was as heart-stoppingly handsome as I remembered. Better, even. "Etta's missed you."

The hard line softened, and he stepped toward me, making my breath hitch. Dark stubble flecked his jaw, and his short-cropped hair had grown out just enough that it was starting to curl at the edges. Downright shabby by Connor's standards.

"Is that so?" he asked. "Did anyone else you know miss me?"

That was more like it. I noticed his eyes were the exact shade as the overcast sky. Then I remembered I had vomit breath. I rocked back on my heels and surreptitiously stuck my hand in front of my mouth to block the fumes. "Hmm. Nope."

His business face slammed into place. "Where is your client?"

Ugh. How could I have been worried about my feelings and my breath when Earnest was lying dead in this stupid dung heap of an abandoned building? I pointed to the gaping door that looked like it could fall off at any moment.

Connor ducked into his vehicle—a black SUV, of course—and grabbed a flashlight. "Show me."

My legs turned to Jell-O as I once again stepped inside the rat-infested walls, and I felt a stab of guilt for not standing vigil over Earnest's body to keep the little bastards away.

Connor spotted my hesitation at the second doorway and swept past me. I heard squeaks and rustling, but thankfully his broad-shouldered silhouette blocked the view.

"You can go wait outside if you'd like."

I swallowed back bile. "No. I worked with Earnest for months. I might be able to help." I knew Earnest better than Connor ever would. Cared about him more too. Maybe it would give me an edge, let me notice something a stranger would miss. I couldn't flee for my own comfort when Earnest's justice was at stake.

Somehow, though, I couldn't bring myself to step forward either.

Connor squatted beside the body and put on a pair of gloves. "There's tissue damage around the needle marks in his arm as well as some antemortem bruising which could be consistent with a forced injection." He patted the pockets. "Phone and wallet are missing, so he might have been mugged, or someone was trying to make it look like he was. It's also possible the items were looted by a third-party postmortem." He pulled out a piece of paper.

"A receipt for . . . Cheetos Bolitas? Purchased a bit before one thirty this morning."

"They were his favorite," I said. They were a spicy flavor of Cheetos made for the Mexican market and only sold at a few specific stores locally. "He finished his last packet yesterday, and I promised I'd pick up some more for him this morning, but I was running late and . . ."

He'll never eat them again.

"He was agoraphobic right? I doubt he wandered out and bought them in the middle of the night just because he'd run out."

I wasn't surprised Connor knew this. He would've been briefed by the Taste Society's research team on the way. They were a group of mysterious tech experts that managed client and personnel data and dug up any information that was asked of them from an undisclosed location.

And Connor was right. It didn't make sense. What the hell had happened last night?

He got to his feet. "I don't want to disturb the scene any more before we can get a team out to go over it properly. It's possible he overdosed without any help, but it warrants investigation."

He steered me back out to the daylight and made some phone calls.

I concentrated on not vomiting. Was I feeling sick at the sight of Earnest's body again? Or was it disgust at my cowardice for not getting closer to see if I could learn anything? I pictured my childhood best friend, Lily, flapping her skinny arms up and down, making chicken noises.

Connor put his phone away. "Police Commander Hunt of the LAPD is on his way. He'll want to talk to you since you discovered the body and would've been one of the last people to see him alive."

I was glad for the distraction. "Police Commander Hunt? Does that mean the Taste Society won't be handling the case?"

"No, it means we'll be cooperating with the LAPD. We don't have a choice when there's a fatality. They won't open an investigation unless the autopsy demonstrates a suspicious death, though, so we'll have a head start."

I thought he'd said cooperating, but the last sentence sounded like he meant competing. My phone rang before I could point this out to him.

"Oh no." My heart parachute jumped out of my ribcage. It was Mrs. Dunst. "Earnest's mom is wondering whether I've found him. What do I tell her?"

Connor grabbed the phone from me and turned it off. "We'll let the police tell her. They'll be here soon."

"But we were supposed to meet. And she told me to search here. What if she comes looking for me?"

"Then we'll deal with it if she does."

I felt the urge to heave again, but there was nothing left in my stomach. "She deserves to know." My voice cracked. She'd looked after him for the past twenty-nine years of her life. My grief would be nothing compared to hers. She needed to know.

Connor wiped my cheek, and I discovered it was wet again. "She'll know soon enough. And you shouldn't have to break the news. You can tell her the police wouldn't let you answer your phone." His knuckles grazed my other cheek. "I'll see if I have a handkerchief in the car."

He returned a moment later and passed me an immaculate, pressed white handkerchief. After a prick of regret at ruining it, I mopped up my tears and blew my nose before it could start producing snot bubbles.

"That's some hay fever you've got there," Connor said when I was done. "I didn't realize you were allergic to the Christmas season."

I stuffed the handkerchief in my pocket, not about to give it back in its current condition. "Did you just make a joke?"

"I don't know. You'd have to tell me the definition of one first."

That was definitely a joke. Not a very good one, but still. "Are you trying to cheer me up?"

He patted my shoulder. "Just making sure you represent the Taste Society in the best possible light to Commander Hunt."

DESPITE CONNOR'S good intentions, Police Commander Hunt was utterly unimpressed. He was a combination of tough cowboy and ex-military man, with a steel-gray buzz cut, sun-weathered face, and bristly mustache that'd stab you if you came too close. I got the impression he could kill without blinking and probably ate rawhide for breakfast. He made his way over to us with a lazy, controlled swagger and sized me up like I was a mound of horse manure.

"The first thing most people do when they find a dead body is call the police," he informed me. "So you must be yet another recruit of the bloody Taste Society." His frown told me plenty of what he thought about that.

"It's just the Taste Society, Commander," Connor said.

"I'll bear that in mind, Stiles. Now what the hell do we have here?"

"Come see for yourself. Isobel, you might as well stay outside."

I felt like chewed-up and spat-out rawhide, so I took the reprieve and slunk to my car, which was boxed in by Connor's SUV and Hunt's police cruiser. Connor had kept my phone, which meant I couldn't call Mrs. Dunst back even if I could've summoned the wherewithal to do it. Instead, I stared at nothing and wished I could start the day over. Two days over. Last night, Earnest had asked if I wanted to stay up late and watch the new *Star Wars* movie with him. He'd even offered to make me a nest out of his comforter and pillows, knowing how much I liked to snuggle up in the cooler weather. What if I'd stayed? I'd been tired, but I could've fallen asleep on the couch. Would he still be alive?

I used Connor's hanky again.

He and Commander Hunt came out about ten minutes later. I scrambled out of the car and stood at attention before I realized what I was doing.

Hunt's focus zeroed in on me. "Unless the coroner reports otherwise, the LAPD will regard this death the way it appears. An overdose by a known drug addict. Nevertheless, as the person who might've seen him last and discovered the body, I'd like you to come down to the station at some point today and give your statement."

"Why not let her give it to you here and now?" Connor asked.

The commander's attention didn't leave me. "You got better things to do this afternoon? Like hide the evidence maybe?"

It took a second for his words to filter through my miasma of misery. "Wha—" I shook my head hard enough to make me dizzy. "No, sir."

"That's commander to you, and don't you forget it. Now

I need to go break the news to his poor mother. Stay out of trouble." His glare shifted to Connor. "The both of you. Any enquiries you make, Stiles, you make under your own PI name. None of this police consultant shit unless we open an official investigation, got it?"

Connor nodded. "Not my first rodeo, Commander." Apparently I wasn't the only one who thought Hunt was cowboy-esque.

The cowboy swaggered to his unmarked police vehicle and drove off without a backward glance. All that was missing was a horse and a sunset. And justice for Earnest.

"So, what do you think of our top-secret LAPD liaison?"

It was part of how the authorities covered up the underground poison scene, along with the existence of the Taste Society. Only a few select law enforcement agents in each precinct were in the know, and they made sure to oversee the relevant cases. I didn't miss his emphasis on "top secret," either, a reminder to keep my mouth shut.

"Cuddly as a shoebox full of kittens," I said. "He seems to like you a bunch. What did you do to him?"

"Same as you. Work for the Taste Society." He paused for a beat. "And solve a whole lot of cases before he could."

Let the chest puffing begin. I wasn't in the mood for egos or politics, but a bit of healthy competition might increase the chances of finding Earnest's killer. If he hadn't killed himself that is. I shoved the thought aside, refusing to believe it. Somehow it would make his death even more tragic. I blinked to hold back tears and then blinked again before remembering my focus-on-the-case strategy. "Where do we start?"

Connor assessed me. His wintry-gray eyes were positively gooey compared to Hunt's ice-blue ones. "What makes you think there's a 'we'?"

"Common sense. You can't chase up Earnest's known enemies without something to go on, and right now we don't even know for sure he's been murdered. Seems like you need to work out whether he was abducted or left the apartment of his own free will while you wait for the autopsy and tox results. Which means you'll start at his home to look for indicators, and it'd be helpful to have someone along who can tell you if anything's out of place."

"Have you been studying?"

I had been, kind of. I'd had a lot of time to read while Earnest was on his computer, and I'd accidentally gravitated toward PI detective stories. Standing next to Connor now had me hoping there weren't any Freudian implications behind my newfound interest.

"You did once tell me that I'm a quick learner," I hedged.

"Well, you're almost right. First, we're going to pay a visit to the convenience store where Earnest bought his Cheetos. You can follow me there, but don't get any ideas about staying on the case." His gaze raked over me, and

I wondered if he was appreciating the view or marveling that he'd ever found me attractive. "I'd hate for it to become a habit."

He was leaning against his black SUV, a picture of stunning, unruffled perfection despite his time in the rat- and spider-infested darkness with a dead body and grumpy police commander. Being in his vicinity for the past hour had made me flustered and self-conscious in all sorts of ways I hadn't felt in months. I didn't like it.

"Me too," I agreed.

I wasn't sure if I was lying.

3

THE KID BEHIND THE COUNTER at Diego's Convenience Store hadn't been working at one thirty in the morning, but he was happy to let us watch the security footage. "Have Yourself a Merry Little Christmas" played in the background as Connor fast-forwarded to the time stamp on the Cheetos receipt.

We watched a grainy image of Earnest enter the store. His posture and movements portrayed nervousness. But there wasn't enough detail to see whether he was under the influence of anything, and since he looked nervous whenever he left his home, it was hard to glean much from it. Except that he was alone.

Unless his abductor had known about the security camera and forced him to go in alone. But why would they make him buy Cheetos Bolitas? It made no sense. And when he took the receipt, it seemed as if he smiled for a second. In anticipation of the cheese-flavored goodness? Or because he was high as a kite and thought the guy behind the counter looked like a buxom beauty in one of those skintight sci-fi suits he found so appealing? Impossible to tell.

Connor made a sneaky copy of the footage, just in case, and we left the back room. "When's the guy who was working last night's graveyard shift scheduled next?" he asked the helpful kid behind the counter.

I winced. *Poor word choice.*

"Tonight, from midnight," the kid said.

We thanked him and agreed to travel the two blocks to Earnest's place in convoy. Judging by the way my elasticized waistband was digging in, I should've walked. But I excused myself by reasoning that two blocks wouldn't have touched the extra pounds anyway.

I'm pretty sure it's that kind of logic that leads to the downfall of resolutions everywhere.

Connor turned off route. I flashed my high beams at him to let him know he was lost, but he didn't stop until we arrived at a bakery.

I pulled in behind him, and he came over to my window. "Has it been long enough since you worked at Bakers Bliss that you can enjoy a jelly-filled donut, or should we go somewhere else?" he asked.

I opened my mouth and shut it again without any words coming out.

"You've had a rough morning. From what I remember, you're partial to comfort food, right?"

My heart swelled like a bread roll you dropped in the lake. Before it was devoured by the ducks. I was so touched that I had to fight back tears. You know it's been a bad day when the offer of a jelly donut makes you cry.

"A jelly-filled donut sounds great," I said.

We sat at one of the two tables the bakery had out front. There was a chill in the air, but I didn't feel like being cooped up inside. Connor surprised me by buying a donut for himself as well. Somehow he managed to eat it without getting powdered sugar everywhere. He waited until I'd finished licking sugar off my own face and fingers before speaking.

"Tell me what happened this morning."

I told him.

He listened studiously, jotting the odd note in the battered spiral-bound notepad he carried around for this purpose. I never had figured out why he used that over the expensive leather version I'd first expected.

When I got to the part about visiting the drug dens, he laid the notepad on the table. Maybe to avoid crushing it. "Please tell me you didn't go alone."

"Um."

"Or that you at least carried pepper spray to protect yourself. Tasers don't always work on drug users."

"Well . . ."

"Shit, Avery. Didn't I teach you anything?"

He sounded upset. It took a lot to make Connor upset.

"Sorry." I didn't have the experience to know it was that dangerous. The only drug use I'd seen firsthand was people smoking weed at parties, and I'd been too worried about Earnest to stop and think about how different that was.

He spread a hand over his face. "Sure. That's what I'll tell Etta and Oliver and your parents when you wind up dead." His hand dropped, and we both waited until his normal calm expression returned. "Right. Finish the story."

I got through the rest without further incident. Connor offered to buy me something else from the bakery, but I declined. The food and debrief had shored me up, and I felt less breakable. Time to get on with it.

The white painted brick exterior of Earnest's apartment building stood unchanged from the morning's events. Connor handed me a pair of latex gloves. "Let's do a methodical search for anything out of place."

I used my spare key again, and we slipped inside.

The familiar, stuffy, yet not unpleasant scent of Earnest's apartment hit me like a brick to the face. Salty and artificial, like stale junk food. At least when an animal hadn't died in the crawl space below anyway, which happened more often than you might think.

Earnest wouldn't have to deal with that again. Because he wouldn't ever come home again. Falling apart wouldn't help though, so I ignored the tightness in my throat and scanned the narrow entry hall. Empty coatrack for his infrequent guests. Fan poster of the *Firefly* crew and a second one of *StarCraft*. Black umbrella propped in the corner where it had sat unused, possibly for years, seeing as it almost never rained in LA and Earnest leaving the house was an even rarer phenomenon. I hadn't thought about how extraneous it was. I would've teased him about it if he were here. Another painful pang.

We went to the bedroom next, Connor a comforting and distracting presence at my back. As cool and impassive as he tended to be, we'd developed a camaraderie that bordered on something more when our jobs had forced us to spend every waking moment together. Then our assignments had wrapped up, and he'd walked out of my life and disappeared.

Of all the times I'd thought about seeing him again, I'd never considered it might take a tragedy to make it happen.

I returned my focus to the task at hand, drawing strength from the walls that had kept Earnest penned and protected for the past three years. You wouldn't know he was rich by the way he lived. Before his spiral into anxiety and addiction, he'd had a stressful, lucrative job as a programmer and had designed an iPhone app on the side that set him up for life. But his apartment was budget middle-class fare and sparsely furnished except for the who-knows-how-many thousands of dollars of technological equipment. He didn't even own the place, just rented it.

If I had that kind of money, I'd need a bigger house to fit all my coffee equipment in. Some people fantasize about BDSM. I fantasize about properly roasted, freshly extracted espresso.

Earnest's bedroom wasn't a space I'd spent much time in. Without any witnesses, there'd been no point in sleeping over to maintain my girlfriend cover. His queen-size bed was neatly made. Because he hadn't pulled off the covers to make a nest for me. Because I'd skipped the movie and gone home. Because I'd abandoned him. There was no evidence of him using it last night.

Nothing on his bedside table except a bunch of cords to charge his various devices. I hadn't paid that much attention, but it seemed right. More sci-fi posters adorned the walls. A small bookshelf filled with computer coding and hacking books that made my eyes cross over even trying to make sense of the titles.

I moved to his wardrobe. Identical black T-shirts hung on wire coat hangers. No surprises there. I'd never seen him wear anything else. A stacked pile of shorts, black as well, sat next to a few pairs of jeans. His underwear was the only splash of color and featured more sci-fi paraphernalia. I suspected his mom bought them for him seeing as there was no way he would have chosen the Iron Man pair. The thought of his scrawny, pasty frame in the red "armor-plated" undies almost made me smile.

A lonely suit hung at the very rear of the wardrobe. I wondered how long it had been since he'd worn it and whether he'd wear it at his funeral. I shut the wardrobe door and locked that thought in there with it.

"All seems normal so far," I reported to Connor, who was standing too close behind me. He laid a steadying hand on my back, like he knew how fragile I felt inside. Or like maybe he was glad to see me again too. Then he stepped aside, and we made our way into the en-suite.

What I wouldn't give to walk in and find Earnest on the toilet.

Not a Christmas wish I'd ever expected to have.

But like this morning, it was empty of both people and clues. As was the kitchen, laundry, and dining room, although there might have been a mouse in the pantry. It reminded me of Meow, and I had the strongest urge to race home and find comfort in her soft fur, rumbling purrs, and vicious delight in chasing roaches.

I'd subconsciously saved the most likely room for last.

The living area doubled as Earnest's work and gaming station, and if he hadn't gone to bed, chances were he'd been sitting here until he'd left or been abducted. It was also the room I knew best, as I usually hung out on the couch reading when I wasn't cooking or eating. I scanned the space carefully, wishing I'd paid more attention or had spy training so I'd remember random stuff like this. And so I could do jujitsu.

Two computers and three large monitors angled around his desk in their usual positions and were plugged into the backup power supply underneath. A precaution against the building's faulty wiring that kept tripping despite two call outs by an electrician. Brightly wrapped Christmas presents and a bowl of candy canes occupied the back left corner. Those were compliments of Mrs. Dunst. She thought it was too sad to have no decorations at all but also knew the only kinds her son would care for.

My throat ached from holding in my grief.

Earnest was compulsively neat, except for junk food and its corresponding rubbish which somehow escaped the radar. As I looked over his workstation again, I remembered with embarrassment that the three Cheetos Bolitas packets and four candy cane wrappers on his desk were all eaten yesterday by the two of us.

At least Connor couldn't tell when they were eaten. Or so I hoped.

The important takeaway was, it didn't seem like Earnest had eaten anything without me. Which meant it was unlikely that he'd unwittingly consumed drugs that might affect his behavior. But his mouse was half off its pad.

"There." I pointed. "Earnest wouldn't have left his mouse that way. Not under normal circumstances."

Connor eyed the desk, littered with wrappers, dubiously. "Are you sure?"

"Yes."

"Was his mouse like that when you came looking for him this morning?"

I cursed my lack of spy training again. "I don't know."

"Right. Well it's not much to go on, but it's a start I guess. I'll call in the team and see what they can find on his computers. Given his whistle-blowing website, that's our best bet."

"It's also pretty much the one place he interacted with the outside world," I pointed out.

"Speaking of the outside world, as Earnest's grieving girlfriend, you better go and pay a visit to Mrs. Dunst."

My chest hurt when I thought of her. "Okay. Then what?"

"Then you maintain your cover and leave the case to me." His face was its customary blank mask, with none of the understanding I'd credited him for earlier.

"But I can help. I know Earnest. I might've seen something important—"

"I've got your number if I need it," he said, dismissing me.

I had a few suggestions for what he could do with that number, but I walked out the front door before I verbalized them. Could my inside knowledge really help find Earnest's killer? Or was I convincing myself of that as a way of avoiding my sorrow?

It couldn't just be an excuse to spend time with Connor again.

I wiped the scowl off my face when I saw the neighbor from the other ground-floor apartment in the tiny shared garden. We'd chatted a few times, and I knew he had two jobs and an elderly mother he cared for that had him coming and going at odd hours. He might have noticed something. "Hi, Humphrey, have you seen Earnest lately?"

He was gently transferring delicate seedlings into the turned-over soil, and I stopped to watch. The slow, methodical movements showed a different side to the man I usually saw rushing in or out. He was fifty going on eighty, his face prematurely creased, and his wide shoulders bent under the strain of too many demands and insufficient time. Because he was a good half foot taller than me, this was also the first occasion I'd had to notice his hair was thinning on top.

"Yes, actually. I saw him last night." He patted the soil down around one seedling and moved to the next. "Or this morning, I should say, if you can call one a.m. morning." He looked up with a shy smile. "Sorry, you don't mind if I keep working do you? I need to head out in half an hour."

"No, of course not. Do you have any idea what he was doing up and about at one a.m.?" I tried not to show how desperately I wanted to know the answer to that question.

He lifted another seedling from the planter box. "I didn't ask, but he seemed to be heading out."

"Was he with anyone?"

"I don't think so. At least, not that I saw."

That didn't seem possible. Unless he fell off the wagon. Which would mean his death really was a tragic overdose. "How sure are you? Did you see him clearly?"

"Well, it was dark and I'd been helping Mother, so I was tired too, but I'm pretty sure since I was so surprised." He peered up at me. "Earnest moved in, what, a few years ago? But I've only seen him out of his apartment a handful of times and never alone."

I pasted a smile on my face. "Well, thanks very much for your help. I'll keep looking then."

He waved me a grubby goodbye, and I wondered whether to tell Connor what I'd learned or let him do his own damn legwork seeing as he'd just kicked me off the case.

I also wondered what could have compelled Earnest to break his fifteen months of sobriety and use heroin . . . or break all precedent and leave his apartment alone without it.

FOR EARNEST'S SAKE, I texted Connor what Humphrey had said. Then I focused on steeling myself for what was ahead and drove to Mrs. Dunst's house, picking up flowers on the way. I'd been to her home a few times before to drop off or collect things for Earnest. She still mothered him in every way he'd let her, and she'd welcomed me with open arms, delighted that her son had met someone who accepted him, agoraphobia, drug addict past and all.

As I stepped up to the timber and stained glass front door, lilies in hand, I'd never felt like such a fraud.

"Izzy, oh darling, come here." She pulled me into her ample bosom. "They told me you found him. You poor thing. I can't believe he's gone." Her bosom heaved against me in giant sobs, and my chest ached in response.

"I'm so sorry, Mrs. Dunst." I hugged her tightly. "So sorry."

She got the heaving under control and pulled back, wiping the tears away briskly. "Oh and you brought flowers. How lovely of you. Come in, come in. I'll find a vase for them."

"I don't want to intrude at such a painful time. I just wanted to pay my respects and drop these off."

"Nonsense. You're not intruding, and I'd welcome the company. You loved him too."

Her words made me even more uncomfortable, but I couldn't leave her on her own if she wanted someone to mourn with. She wiped her eyes again, and I wished I had a clean handkerchief to offer her. Connor would've had another one. Maybe because he wasn't very competent at offering comfort through other means. Or maybe because he was in the habit of making people cry.

"Can I make you a cup of tea while you're getting a vase?" I asked.

"Oh. Yes, that would be nice, thank you." She grabbed a tissue from a box on the hallway stand and blew her nose. "I don't know what I'm going to do without him, you know?"

"I know." It was painfully easy to understand. Her life orbited around his. Only yesterday, I'd been talking to Earnest about whether we could convince her to take a holiday while I took over some of her caretaker jobs. It felt like forever.

I rattled through the honey-colored oak cabinets for mugs and tea bags. The cozy warmth of the timber seemed too cheerful for the occasion, the neatly stacked shelves too ordered. The grinning squirrel canister that guarded the sugar would benefit from being dropped on the floorboards.

Mrs. Dunst watched me without seeing. "I can't work out why he fell off the wagon. He had you, after all, and he was less anxious lately."

Probably because he had me, but not for the reasons she thought. "I guess something might have happened with his job?" I didn't know what else to say. My gut said Earnest didn't kill himself, but I wasn't going to mention the possibility of foul play. Not until the police had concrete evidence.

She huffed. "That website of his. I'll never wrap my head around why he thought it was a good idea. Why focus on conspiracies and deceit if you have an anxiety disorder?"

I handed her the cup and took the lilies she was still clutching. The long stems looked bruised.

"I think he saw it as important. His way of making a difference to the world, even though he couldn't enter into it." I plonked the flowers in a jug of water. It would do for now. "Why don't we sit down?"

She allowed me to lead her to the glass dining table and sat when I pulled out a chair.

"You really got to know him well in a short time," she said. "Maybe understood him in a way I never could. Would you . . . would you help me plan the funeral?"

My guilt hurtled upward like a well-shot spitball. "Oh, Mrs. Dunst, I couldn't. I mean, I only knew him for a few months. You've looked after him and loved him his whole life. I'd feel like an impostor." All true. Especially the last part.

"No, you'd be nothing of the sort. I'd appreciate it. And I think it's what Earnest would have wanted."

Crap. How could I say no to that?

She reached out and grabbed my hand. "Please, Izzy?"

"Okay. If you're sure that's what you want, I'd be happy to help."

Her face lit up, and my heart shriveled a little inside me. I was a horrible fraud, and I was going to hell.

4

I COULDN'T FACE Commander Hunt's scorn when I was already feeling wretched, so I decided to delay giving my statement until tomorrow. I drove home, trying not to think about Earnest, or about Mrs. Dunst, or about the funeral.

I trudged up the two flights of stairs to my apartment. It was outdated and tatty, but familiar and comfortable like an old favorite sweater, and I couldn't wait to get inside.

My key was out, ready to go, and I was concentrating on the hot shower I was going to take and the novel I was going to escape into with Meow curled by my side. But as I walked past Etta's door, I heard a deep rumble of laughter that made me lose control of the motor function in my legs.

I regained control in time to stop myself collapsing and peeked in the window. Sure enough, Mr. Black was squeezed into one of Etta's recliners.

The recliner looked like it was about to explode at the seams under his incredible bulk, and I wouldn't blame it one bit. It put the traitor button on my jeans in a whole new light; never mind that his bulk was mostly muscle. I drew away from the window and leaned against the wall to collect myself.

I hadn't told Etta what Mr. Black did for a living. To be fair, I thought I'd seen the last of him. I took a few calming breaths. *Okay,* I told myself. *It's not so bad.* I didn't know what he was doing here, but I was pretty sure it wasn't to bust my kneecaps.

My loan payments were all up to date, thanks to Connor pulling some strings to organize two months of advance pay from the Taste Society. And to Earnest for making the job so easy that I hadn't been fired yet.

I desperately wanted to continue on with my prior plan of shower, book, and bed, but my conscience wouldn't let me. Until Etta knew the truth about Mr. Black, I needed to play chaperone. Not that I knew exactly what might go wrong, or what I'd do to stop it if it did, but it didn't matter. Due diligence and all that.

I stayed squished against the wall as I rummaged through my bag. While I no longer kept the SABRE Red pepper spray on my person at all times, I had taken to carrying it and the Taser in my bag. I'd never be able to retrieve them in time in the event of an actual emergency, but if I was stupidly, knowingly about to put myself in danger, like now, at least I could arm myself first.

Pity about this morning at the drug dens when I was too stupid to even know.

I knocked on the door, and Etta swung it open, her cheeks flushed. Behind her was an apartment that was the mirror image of mine, except hers had been renovated this century. The kitchen and living area were fitted out in white, gray, and turquoise hues. The counters and coffee table were gloss white, the appliances stainless steel, and abstract monochrome prints stood in place of my 1960s tropical wallpaper. There was also a real, tastefully decorated Christmas tree freshening the room with its pine scent.

My housemate, Oliver, was on the charcoal linen sofa opposite Mr. Black, with Dudley's head resting in his lap. They all smiled at me, even Mr. Black. Lucky I'd braced myself before knocking, or I might have had the type of accident it's only acceptable for two-year-olds to have.

"Izzy, so glad you could join us!" Etta chirped. "We're having a welcome party for Dudley. Just a quiet one, of course, so we don't stress him out."

Dudley was still using Oliver as a pillow. His placid response to the ruckus of my arrival was to open one eye and give another of his halfhearted tail wags. I went over to pet him, partly because he was adorable and I couldn't resist, and partly to procrastinate interacting with Mr. Black. "Yep, sure wouldn't want to stress you out, hey boy?" He sighed in satisfaction under my hands.

Oliver grinned at me. He had one of those boyish faces that would've made him a good leading man for Peter Pan, and unkempt, shaggy blond hair that was always flopping into his eyes. Though he was in his midthirties, I liked to tease him about being a bartender who didn't look old enough to drink.

"I heard you carried Dudley up the stairs this morning," he said with the fancy British accent that made every word he uttered seem both dignified and more intelligent than mine. "I would've enjoyed seeing that."

I groaned and rubbed my back. "Have you done the honors yet?"

"Nope, Mr. Black has been kindly helping Etta all day."

I finally looked up at the Hulk himself, shocked as usual by how big he was up close. *Breathe. He's not trying to kill you this time.*

With his tan skin, generous mouth, and soulful brown eyes, Mr. Black was quite attractive if you didn't know what he did for a living. And if you had a thing for shiny-skulled giants with a jagged scar on their left cheek. Which Etta did, apparently.

He gave me a nod. "Nice to see you, Ms. Avery."

I couldn't bring myself to say the same, so I asked, "How's your wife and daughter?" I'd never met them, but as it was for his daughter and the sake of her Disney Princess watch that he hadn't broken my kneecaps, I felt quite fondly toward them.

"Oh, they're both real good. Thanks so much for asking."

"Well, uh, thanks for carrying Dudley all day. I'm not sure my back could've dealt with doing it again."

"It's no trouble. I'm always happy to help out a sweet old lady like Etta."

I saw Etta stiffen in my peripheral vision. "You mean a smoking-hot lady like Etta, right?" I asked.

Etta had been drooling over Mr. Black from day one, and despite the thirty-year age gap, I'd suspected they'd slept together after I spotted him leaving her apartment with his shirt buttons askew. She'd explained away the buttons with some implausible story about a fish tank though, and I'd never known for sure.

Mr. Black scratched his head. "Uh, right."

Wow. The fish tank story was true. I was super glad he was faithful to his wife, but I wasn't certain how to do damage control with Etta. Her posture was still rigid.

Oliver jumped in. "Izzy, before you stopped by, we were talking about bringing Meow over to say hi to Dudley. Do you think you could go get her? I would, but well, you know . . ." He gestured to Dudley's head in his lap.

I turned to Etta. "What do you think? I know you wanted to keep today nice and calm." I thought it was a bad idea, but a distraction was clearly needed.

Etta looked at Dudley, and her shoulders softened. "Well, like you said this morning, he seems pretty relaxed. And it would be good for them to meet. I'm hoping they can be friends since Dudley didn't have much of a chasing instinct, but I'll put him on a leash while they get used to each other."

"I'd like to see your cute cat again," Mr. Black chimed in. "As long as she won't poop in Etta's shoes."

Etta and Oliver's heads swung my way, and I pressed a finger to my lips while Mr. Black looked around the room, probably for shoes. I might have told him a little white lie about Meow's pooping preferences, but it was for a good cause. He'd been thinking of taking her home as a kind of safety deposit to make sure I'd come through on my end of a deal we'd struck.

"Okay. I'll go get her then, I guess." I returned a few minutes later, Meow in my arms. This time when I came through the door, Dudley's head shot up.

Etta tightened her grip on his leash.

Meow thrashed her way out of my grasp and leaped onto the top of Mr. Black's recliner. Her fur looked like she'd put her paw in a light socket, and she was hissing like the leaky radiator in my former junk heap of a car.

For a split second I thought she was protesting Mr. Black's presence and was mentally congratulating her for being the only one with discernment when I followed her slitty gaze and saw Dudley quivering behind Etta's legs. He must have flown off the couch as soon as Meow moved. "Um, Oliver, do you know if Meow has any history with dogs?"

"Nope, she's a rescue so . . . crap, you're bleeding!" Yes, even the word crap sounded dignified.

I looked down at my arms. He was right. I was bleeding. Not all that much, but Meow had gotten in a couple of good, deep scratches.

"Oh dear, you better see a doctor for that," Etta said. "Cat's claws can have all sorts of nasties in them." She patted the still trembling Dudley. His tail was tucked so far under him that it almost reached his front legs. "I might get him out of sight so they can both calm down some, and then you better take her home again."

Lucky me.

Dudley shadowed Etta into another room, and Meow shrank down to her normal dainty self. With her gray fur and bold black stripes, I'd always thought she looked like a miniature white tiger that had been playing in the fireplace. Judging by my ribboned flesh, she'd hold her own in the grasslands of Southeast Asia.

"Sorry, Iz, I can take her," Oliver said, springing to his feet.

I gave Meow a few cautious strokes, and she started purring. I took that as a sign it was safe to pick her back up. "No, it's okay. I might as well take her and get myself cleaned up."

He squeezed past me and scooped her up anyway. "I'll help then." Maybe he was feeling guilty. Or maybe he didn't want me to bleed on Meow.

Ten minutes later, I returned to Etta's apartment, smelling of antiseptic. Meow was smugly eating a second dinner, and Oliver was getting ready for work.

I found Etta on the landing, a cigarette between her fingers. "Why are you out here all alone?"

She breathed out a lungful of smoke. "Now I've got Dudley, I'm making myself come outside. I don't want him to have any ill effects from the secondhand tobacco." She inhaled one last time before stubbing it out. "Let's head in."

Dudley was on the couch, looking like his usual chilled self. The hulking menace of Mr. Black was missing.

"Where's Mr. Black?" I asked, my neck prickling as I pictured him coming up behind me.

"He wasn't feeling well, so he went home. Doesn't like the sight of blood, apparently."

My jaw fell. "That's impossible!"

Etta eyed me. "Nothing impossible about it at all. It's a common phobia."

Oh boy. If I was ever going to tell her the truth about Mr. Black, now was the time. And I had to tell her, or Mr. Black would become a repeat guest around here. If she forgave him for calling her old, that is. But would she forgive me for not telling her in the first place?

"Why are you pacing about all worked up like that? I hope you didn't catch some weird disease from that cat scratch."

Ugh. I sat down abruptly. "Etta, I have to tell you something about Mr. Black. He was never my personal trainer like you assumed—"

"You were cheating on Connor?"

"What? No. I owe money to some, uh, unsavory characters, and when I first moved in, I'd been out of work and unable to pay them for a while. Mr. Black was here on their behalf to, you know, motivate me."

"You mean he's a bruiser for some debt collector?" She nodded to herself. "Sure, I can see that."

I searched her face. She didn't look anywhere near freaked out enough. "So you understand why you need to stay away from him right?"

"Nope, now you've lost me."

"Because he's dangerous. Because he breaks bones for a living."

"Pfft. Are you telling me you've never had a job you're not proud of? A person's job isn't who they are, and Abe never broke any of your bones, so I'm not sure why you're giving him such a hard time about it. Seems he was real nice to you considering, and he's always been sweet to me."

"Wait. Abe?"

"Yes, Abe. Short for Abraham. Sheesh, you're telling me you don't even know his first name, and you're prancing about on your high horse telling me to stay away from him?"

"But—"

"Besides"—she smirked—"how dangerous can he be if he's scared of a little blood?"

I hung my head. This conversation was not going how I'd planned. Actually, she was kind of arguing me around to her point of view, but I hadn't forgotten my terror-stricken encounters with him. My dreams wouldn't let me forget. I decided to play dirty. "Didn't I hear him call you a sweet old lady tonight?"

Etta struck me with a scowl that might've sent me running if I hadn't been so exhausted. "That was low, Izzy, even for you."

"I'm sorry, but I'm worried about you."

"Piffle. I've survived close to three quarters of a century on this crazy Earth, and I'm not about to be afraid of some family-oriented bruiser who's too nice to do his job properly! And for the record, it wasn't the old part I objected to. Hell, I know I'm old, and I'm proud of it. It's annoying at times, when my body isn't as fit as it used to be, but it has its benefits too, like I can say whatever I want and no one will naysay me." She shot me a meaningful look. "It was the word 'sweet' that got to me. Sweet is just so . . . insipid, so boring. I'm not boring."

"Boring is the last thing I'd describe you as," I said truthfully. "But didn't you describe Mr. Black as sweet earlier?" Calling him Abe felt wrong.

She flicked her hand at me dismissively. "That was in a very different context."

I didn't naysay her.

AFTER I'D LEFT Etta and Dudley snuggling on the couch, all I wanted to do was crawl into bed and bring this never-ending crappy day to an end. But Etta had made me promise to get antibiotics for the cat scratches, and considering she was the type of person to think gator hunting was fun and giant bruisers were sweet, I figured I should take it seriously.

I phoned my handler Jim and went through the usual identification rigmarole. "How do I go about seeing a doctor for . . . non-poison-related needs?"

"You call me, and I organize it for you. Because I don't have anything better to do with my Friday night."

"Uh. Okay. Can you do that then?"

He grunted. "Anything for you." Then he hung up.

What a nice guy he was.

The mystery novel I'd been reading felt too close to home, so I scrounged through Oliver's books and found a comedy by David Sedaris. An hour later, I was learning about the recreational uses of catheters when I heard a knock on the front door. I dragged on my Ugg boots over my cupcake flannel pajamas and unlocked the deadbolt to find Dr. Levi Eduardo Reyes standing there. He was the doctor who'd tended to me on three separate occasions when I'd been poisoned or shot. His beauty threatened to upstage Connor's. Toffee skin, molten chocolate eyes, and wicked dimples.

Damn.

Those eyes skimmed over me and my pajamas, and I caught a glimpse of the dimples before he bowed. "Madam, I'm here to rescue you." His Hispanic accent was faint, just enough to add interest. He straightened up and gestured at the *Chrismyass* poster on the other side of the door. "Although I hope I don't have to kiss Santa's ass to do it. How can I help?"

"Sorry, no kissing required, and I should've told J— my handler it wasn't an emergency. I didn't mean to drag you out so late."

"It's fine. No problem at all, as long as you let me in anyway." He rubbed his bare arms. "It's cold out here."

I stepped aside. "Only someone who lives in California could make that claim in sixty degrees. Would you like a cup of tea to warm you up?"

"I'd love one, thanks." He watched me as I shuffled around the kitchen. "So, I know last time I saw you I said we had to stop meeting like this, but I have to admit, there's a part of me that was disappointed you hadn't been poisoned or shot lately."

Startled, I glanced his way and saw his eyes twinkling with mischief. I threw a cookie at him without thinking. A side effect of living with Oliver. "That's the creepiest thing I've heard for a while."

He caught the cookie and bit into it. "It was supposed to be romantic. You know, heartwarming."

"You need to work on that." I carried our two steaming mugs, milk, sugar, and a plate of cookies over to the dining table. "Why don't we sit down?"

"You must have been a waitress in a former life."

"Close enough, a barista." More than a barista, actually. Coffee and food were two of my greatest passions, and I'd opened my own beautiful coffee shop right before the stock market, a bad loan, and my marriage all crashed and burned at once. The coffee shop had gone up in the merry, metaphorical flames. "What about you?"

He sipped his tea, leaned back in his chair, and closed his eyes momentarily, his long eyelashes in full display against his cheeks. "That's better, thanks." He rested the cup on the table. "I served as an Army emergency physician."

I scanned his unkempt hair and ever-ready dimples. "Really? I can't imagine you in the Army."

"Well, I got out as soon as I could. They didn't appreciate my brilliant wit."

I smiled. "That I can imagine."

He drank some more and looked me over. "What can I do for you?"

"Well . . ." I studied the contents of my mug.

"You can tell me, you know. I'm a doctor."

I could hear the humor in his voice, but it didn't help. It had seemed embarrassingly minor *before* I'd learned he used to treat war wounds. "It's nothing much." I looked up. "I probably don't even need a doctor."

He sipped his tea again, but the mug couldn't hide the laughter in the lines around his eyes. "You could try letting the doctor be the judge of that."

My innards squirmed in anticipated humiliation, but it was too late to back out now. I rolled up my pajama sleeves. "I got scratched by my housemate's cat. My neighbor made me promise I'd get antibiotics for it."

"Does the cat need medical attention too?"

"Nope, I was without a doubt the loser of the skirmish. She's curled up on my pillow after a second helping of dinner."

He bit his lip. To keep from laughing presumably. "Don't be embarrassed. I'd prefer to treat you for something superficial rather than life-threatening."

I held back a retort about how he'd been disappointed by my lack of gunshot wounds.

"Besides, your neighbor is right. A few of those scratches look deep, which means they're hard to clean properly, and cat claws aren't the most hygienic weapons around. You don't want to mess around with bacterial infection."

"Are you only saying that to make me feel better?"

"Nope, I know a woman who was hospitalized after washing her daughter's unappreciative cat. She had a couple of scratches and didn't think anything of it and then woke up the next day with her arm so swollen she couldn't bend it. By the time she made it to hospital, she was feverish and vomiting and had to be put on a penicillin drip."

"You're lying."

"God's honest truth."

I shook my head. “In that case, get me the antibiotics, stat.”

His dimples appeared again. “Yes, doc, right away.” He got to his feet.

“How many drugs do you carry in that van of yours anyway?” I asked.

“Are you planning to break in and steal them to sell on the street?”

“Yes.”

“Thousands of dollars’ worth.”

We smiled at each other, and he ducked outside, returning shortly with my antibiotics. I noticed he wasn’t winded from climbing up and down the stairs that fast, even with his limp.

He handed me the sheet of pills, and I handed him his half-finished tea.

“Take two of these twice a day for five days straight.”

“Two, twice a day?”

“People with your gene mutation need higher doses of drugs for them to have the same effect.” He was talking about the secret gene mutation PSH337PRS, which gave me increased resistance to poisons and was the reason the Taste Society recruited me as a Shade. “Haven’t you ever noticed that painkillers don’t seem to work for you? Or if they work, the relief doesn’t last as long as it’s supposed to?”

I felt my cheeks warm. “Huh. I’d never thought about it.”

"Don't worry. We all assume we're normal until we find out we're not."

"You're not normal?"

"Is anyone working for the Taste Society?" he countered.

"Good point."

He put his mug in the sink and headed toward the door but then stopped and turned. "One last thing."

"Yes?"

"Would you like to go on a date with me?" He was fiddling with the hem of his T-shirt. If I didn't know better, I could've sworn he was nervous.

"What? Why?"

His gorgeous brow furrowed. "Um."

"I mean, why me? Why now?"

He chuckled. "I've wanted to date you from the first time you woke up and told me the counteracting drugs weren't working. I gave you my card, remember?"

"Well, yes, but . . ." After being drugged with a potent aphrodisiac, I'd woken up to find him standing over me, ridiculously good-looking. I'd told him so, certain the aphrodisiac must still be in my system, but as it turned out, he was just that ridiculously good-looking.

When he'd given me his card, I thought it was his gentle way of easing my embarrassment.

"I said I'd like to take you on a date when you came to the medical facility too," Levi reminded me.

When I'd been shot, he meant. Sure, he'd flirted with me, but he'd flirted with the ancient crone in the bed next to me as well.

Except Levi hadn't seemed nervous then. "But this is the first time I could ask you out seriously," he said, his hand returning to the hem of his T-shirt. "Without worrying your judgment was clouded by drugs, that is. So I'm asking."

Perhaps I shouldn't have been so surprised, but I'd spent so much of the past two years berating myself for failing at life and trying to keep treading water that I hadn't considered myself a viable dating prospect. It shocked me that someone else might. Actually, I was kind of shocked he even remembered me after a few brief encounters three months ago.

As if reading my mind, he smiled at me. "You don't know how beautiful you are. It's part of your charm."

Charm? It wasn't a term I associated with myself. "You don't know me very well," I told him.

His dimples flashed. "I'd like to change that."

I thought about it. Two years was a long time, and my life and heart were in a whole lot less of a shambles than they had been. Plus my current client was beyond my protection and Connor had kicked me off the case, so I had the opportunity to go out. The fact that Levi was a drop-dead gorgeous doctor who seemed both fun and kind didn't hurt either.

But I couldn't do it. "I'm sorry. I haven't been on a date since my divorce, and my life and mental state are kind of complicated right now."

He smiled again, and I was relieved to see it still reached those molten-chocolate eyes.

"That's okay, I'll ask you later then. Merry Christmas. And maybe stay away from that cat."

He let himself out, and I watched him go, wondering what was wrong with me.

5

I HADN'T BOTHERED to set an alarm the night before, so I woke up late. It didn't matter though. Earnest wasn't waiting for me.

The shock of that hit me afresh. A night's sleep hadn't dulled the pain, and it punched a hole through my gut. There were twenty-six alerts on my phone encouraging me to hurry up and rush to Earnest's. The most recent said:

You know that saying: "Better to be late than to arrive ugly?" It's not true.

I didn't know whether to laugh or cry. To switch the app off or leave it in honor of him. How could he be gone? Someone had to answer for it. But Connor wasn't waiting for me either. The case was out of my hands. What was I going to do with myself today?

I made a mental list: One, give my statement to Police Commander Hunt. Two, carry Dudley up and down the stairs. Three, help Mrs. Dunst plan Earnest's funeral. I groaned and pulled my pillow over my head.

The pillow failed to block out the sound of someone knocking on the front door. With another groan, I dragged on my Ugg boots, and wearing the same cupcake pajamas, topped off with my slept-in electrocuted zombie hair, trudged over to see who it was.

My day's plans went from bad to the stuff of nightmares.

"Aunt Alice. Henrietta. What a—"

"Surprise." Aunt Alice looked over my rumpled appearance with a level of disdain she reserved for people who stole from the church collection plate, cannibalistic serial killers, and me. "I can tell."

Our eyes were the same shade of blue, but there the resemblance ended. Her chestnut-going-on-gray hair was flawless, pulled back in an elegant French twist, and her blouse and slacks as wrinkle-free as the most Botox-loving celebrity, despite the likelihood that she'd just hopped off an airplane. Her face had been allowed to age gracefully but was enhanced through the artful application of makeup, and her lips were drawn thin in the aforementioned disdain.

Henrietta, Aunt Alice's adult daughter and my least favorite cousin, didn't have the half a century of experience to lend authority to it, but she did a pretty damn good job of imitating her mother's expression.

"I suppose this means you didn't get my emails," Aunt Alice said. "I sent the first over two weeks ago, and another last week, and another yesterday."

I hadn't checked my emails in about a month. I always Skyped my family and best friend in Australia, so the only emails I received were reminders from the loan shark I owed money to, the occasional loose end to tie up from my ex-husband, and amazing deals on penis enlargement from Super Wow Special Store.

The penis ones were my favorite since at least they contained good news. Needless to say, I didn't check my email very often.

"I guess they must have gotten lost," I said lamely.

Aunt Alice cast a pointed gaze over my disheveled state again. "Well, it doesn't look like you have any plans this weekend anyway, so you'll be free to show us the sights of LA."

I cursed every fate that had conspired against me to make that true. Then I decided to lie. "Well, actually—"

"But let's plan the itinerary over refreshments. Aren't you going to invite us in?"

I willed my teeth to stop grinding and stepped aside to let them enter.

"And for goodness' sake, Isobel, what is that monstrosity

doing on your door? I was almost hoping I had the wrong address."

"I guess my housemate has an odd sense of humor," I mumbled, retreating to the kitchen to make tea and dig up some cookies. I had no desire to witness their reaction to our humble apartment. As the kettle boiled, I thought about closing Oliver's bedroom door to keep out the noise, but he was a heavy sleeper. Plus there was a sly, optimistic part of me that hoped he'd wake up and come to my rescue. Or at least that Meow might slink out for a visit.

I tried for a pleasant expression as I sat down after serving them. "So I had no idea your around-the-world trip included a stopover in LA. How long are you here for?"

Henrietta's eyes kept flicking toward the Ninja Turtles stickers on the corner of the dining table, and my pleasant expression became more genuine.

"Like I wrote in those emails," Aunt Alice said, "we're here for six days."

I choked on my tea. Trying to conceal it made it worse, and I found myself unable to breathe, eyes watering. Desperate for air, I instinctively inhaled despite the liquid in my throat and then spluttered tea all over the table. I wasn't sure whether to be grateful or disappointed that it missed Henrietta's pastel pink knit top. "Sorry."

"Well really, Isobel," Aunt Alice chided. "I would've thought after thirty years you'd have mastered the art of drinking."

"I'm still twenty-nine, so maybe there's hope for me yet." I smiled weakly. Neither of them smiled back. "Let me get a washcloth to clean that up."

"How's your new job going?" Aunt Alice asked. "Your mother tells me it's classified?" She sniffed in disapproval. "I can't think what sort of respectable position would be so secretive."

"It's going great," I said. At least it had been until yesterday.

She waved a hand at the apartment, with its musty green carpet, shabby furniture, and the garish feature wall of pineapple, flower, and banana wallpaper, which Oliver had decorated by drawing eyes on half the fruit. "This is temporary then, I take it?"

"I'm saving my money." Even she couldn't argue with that. Never mind that instead of accumulating a nest egg, I was paying it all to the loan shark.

"And do you have a man in your life?" she asked. "I ran into that ex-husband of yours, and he said he's seeing someone."

Just the type of news I want from home. I was homesick sometimes, but never for my ex. Steve was a charming Italian who was fond of cooking his family's secret pasta recipe in nothing but an apron. I used to watch, fantasizing about both the apron and the pasta. Nowadays I fantasized about what I'd do with the kitchen knives he'd taken in the settlement.

I forced myself to answer her question. "No one at the moment. What about you?"

Henrietta's head shot up. Aunt Alice sniffed again, but before she could respond further, fate had a change of heart—or remembered I'd never stolen money from the collection plate—because Oliver stumbled out of the bedroom. He was still pulling his shirt on over his head and was followed closely by Meow.

Aunt Alice saw his naked torso, with its tattoo of eleven tiny birds circling his left shoulder, and cast her eyes away in disapproval. But Henrietta's eyes lingered a little too long. Or had I imagined it?

Oliver blinked a few times as he adjusted to the light, wiped his hair out of his face, and looked over at our guests. "Good morning. Who do we have here?"

"Oliver, meet my aunt Alice and cousin Henrietta." I turned to the women who shared my blood. "Oliver's my housemate," I explained, to stop Aunt Alice assuming I'd lied about the boyfriend thing or that he was some random stranger I liked to have sex with. Not that I'd ever been the type to have sex with random strangers, but Aunt Alice believed I was capable of anything . . . so long as it was bad.

Or something she considered bad. And she considered a *lot* of things bad, so I guess I should've been flattered in a way.

Oliver was looking over Henrietta with appreciation. I tried not to blame him, considering she hadn't opened her mouth yet. She was stunning after all. Long ash-blond hair, determined blue eyes, and lips with the ideal amount of pout. And that was from the neck up. She was also tall and slim with muscle tone she honed at the gym six days a week and accentuated with chaste but flattering designer clothes.

"It's a pleasure to meet you both," he said. "Is this your first time in LA?"

Henrietta nodded. Aunt Alice merely lifted her chin.

"I'm afraid visiting in December doesn't show her off to her full, sunny advantage, but even now she's got England beat by a mile." Oliver had come to Los Angeles for a girl but stayed for the weather. I could understand that; the winter in California was the same temperature as summer in the UK.

"Is that where you're from?" Henrietta asked. "I love your accent."

I was so shocked I almost fell face-first into the bowl of minced cod liver I was preparing for Meow. I'd never heard Henrietta flirt before. I looked up to see her blushing prettily and began to formulate a plan. "Will you two excuse us for a moment?"

I grabbed Oliver and dragged him into my room. "Could you do me a huge favor?" Okay, I felt kind of bad for throwing him to the wolves, but as a bartender, he'd perfected the art of dealing with all personalities and didn't let anything anyone said get to him. I had neither of those skills going for me, so it was more like putting the strongest team member in play. At least they were well-washed wolves with good oral hygiene, which made getting snapped at less unpleasant. Plus I'd bake him a lot of cookies in return.

"Let me guess," he said. "You want me to babysit."

"Well, I've got a lot on today."

He looked at my pajamas. "Obviously."

"And Aunt Alice is my worst nightmare."

"That sounds more like it."

"And I'll cook you whatever you want and clean the house for a week."

"Just one?"

"I caught you admiring Henrietta."

"Make it two."

I held out my hand and we shook. "Deal."

It was the best bargain I had ever made.

I STEPPED INTO the shower on the pretense of getting ready for my oh-so-important day's business while

Oliver herded my nightmare and her daughter out of the apartment. My phone rang when I was lathering shampoo through my hair. Grumbling, I leaned out of the shower to peek at it. Connor.

I wiped my hand on a towel and put the call on loudspeaker, wondering why I still had his number in my phone. It was probably against Taste Society regulations. Personal relationships among Shades were discouraged to make us harder for prospective poisoners to identify, and the same might go for Shades and investigators.

"Change of plans," Connor said. "You're going to be helping me on the case after all. I'll pick you up in fifteen minutes."

He hung up before I could respond. *Jerk.* How did he even know I was home? Had he never gotten rid of that GPS app that allowed him to locate me? And why the change of plans?

Despite his presumptuousness and lack of explanation, my mood lifted. I hoped there weren't any Freudian implications to that either.

I hurried to finish off my shower and considered what to wear. It shouldn't matter, seeing as I'd turned down an invitation to sleep with Connor months ago and wasn't angling for another, but I wanted to look good. Especially after the sweats yesterday. I fought with myself over it and settled on an ivory long-sleeved dress to hide the cat scratches, with stretchy leggings and flat-soled ankle boots. Connor loved heels. So did masochists.

I didn't have time to do any more than swipe some serum through my hair to prevent the electrocuted look and gunk up my eyelashes with mascara. It'd have to do. Somehow I doubted Connor would be impressed.

Ugh. Another thought hit me. How was I going to explain Connor's presence to Etta? I was composing a text asking him to park down the street when I realized Etta was probably waiting for me to carry Dudley down the stairs. Stuff it. I'd think of a way to explain his presence. My back depended on it.

He arrived before I had a chance to shovel any food into me, and I'd left my muffins at Earnest's. This was not my week. I grabbed a banana and tried to convince myself it would be good for me.

I don't mind banana, but I prefer it in pudding or cake.

Etta beat me out onto the landing. "Connor! It's so lovely to see you."

I bet she was finding it lovely. He was wearing his usual PI attire: a tailored shirt (pale gray, today), black dress shoes, and blue jeans that were just the right amount of snug. I saw Etta's eyes dip down as he turned to face me.

"Don't listen to her," I said. "She only wants you to carry Dudley down the stairs." Okay, that's what I wanted, but he didn't need to know he was doing me a favor.

He'd had a haircut, and the stubble was gone. Making me feel even more scruffy. I knew for a fact that he looked equally good in a T-shirt or a suit too.

"Who's Dudley?" he asked.

Etta had left the door open, and Dudley moseyed out. I was gratified that he came to say hi to me first before going up to sniff Connor. "Meet Dudley, Etta's new gentleman companion."

Connor gave Dudley a scratch behind the ear before picking him up. "Where do you want him?"

"Oh, aren't you a dear? Down the bottom of the stairs is fine. He's still learning to navigate them. We got halfway up yesterday, but he seems to find going down harder."

Eighty pounds of couch potato was nothing to Connor. Etta shot me an I-told-you-so look before hurrying to catch up with him. "What brings you here anyway? We've missed seeing you around. Are you and Izzy getting back together?"

"No."

He could have at least hesitated. I rolled my eyes at myself. It's not like we'd ever been going out to begin with.

"We're just friends," I told Etta. "But my company has, uh, hired him for a project, and we'll be working together for some of it."

"What kind of project?"

"The usual kind, meaning confidential," I said.

Connor deposited Dudley onto the sidewalk. Etta clipped on his leash before eyeballing us, one hand on her hip. "You two are no fun at all."

"You have enough fun for the both of us," I retorted and saw her smile as we turned away.

Déjà vu hit hard as I climbed onto the tan leather seats of Connor's SUV, and I had to remind myself not to call him schnookums. I suspected he'd appreciate it even less than he used to after our time apart.

Which meant he'd probably want to push me out the moving vehicle.

"How has your leg healed up?" he asked in reference to my previous encounter with a bullet. The question caught me off guard.

In my surprise, I forgot I was mad at his last-minute phone call. "Oh, fine. I mean, I have a scar that's hard to explain, but it doesn't hurt anymore. How's . . . Maria?" Maria cooked and cleaned for Connor and maybe did more covert duties for him as well. I'd liked her instantly, and not *just* because she was amazing in the kitchen.

"Good. She told me to bring you this." He handed me a thermos, and I realized the car smelled like coffee.

Real, espresso coffee, properly extracted.

I wondered if I was having olfactory hallucinations, if there was such a thing, but my eyes confirmed it. Real coffee.

"How?" I asked. It was a thermos, not a disposable takeout cup, and I couldn't see Maria purchasing an espresso and pouring it into a thermos for me. She had to have made it. But when I'd worked with Connor a few months ago, he'd had a worthless automatic drip machine.

Connor had a thermos too, and he sipped it before answering. "My job is to test out recruits, not be nice to them."

When we'd met, I'd been fresh out of the Taste Society facility where I'd trained to become a Shade, and as far as I'd known, Connor was my first client. Twenty-four hours in, an urgent case had come up that he needed to investigate, so he'd told me the truth: All Shades have a secret, practical assessment to test their competence before being assigned to a real client. He'd been mine, and he'd passed me. Barely.

Now, it took a second for me to make sense of his words, and when I did, I gaped at him incredulously. "Are you saying you acted like a jerk and made me drink filthy drip coffee to—I don't even know—test my mettle or something?"

"The jerk part didn't take much acting." He took another sip and put the thermos in the center console cup holder. "But drinking all that filter coffee damn near killed me."

I snatched his thermos and peered inside. It was real coffee. My brain couldn't come to grips with it. Like trying to unravel a lifetime of being told the world is round, only to find out it's a stew pot for some intergalactic giant. "Holy guacamole," I said at last, too shocked to be mad yet. "You really are dedicated to your job." I let it sink in some more. "No wonder you were such a grump."

Connor grabbed his thermos back. "Like I said, the jerk part was easy."

I remembered to sip my own coffee. The liquid was heavenly. I closed my eyes and leaned back in appreciation. "Tell Maria I love her."

Connor snorted softly.

I gave myself a few minutes of reveling in my espresso before getting down to business. I couldn't believe he'd forced himself to drink, and by extension forced *me* to drink, the insipid coffee-flavored dishwater that was filter coffee for our whole assignment. He'd grimaced, actually grimaced, when I'd made him "try" an espresso. Refused to finish it, in fact. What kind of self-control did this man have? Was he even human? Come to think of it, if he were a cyborg, that would explain a lot.

The cyborg idea was Earnest's influence on me showing through. A sober reminder. "So why am I back on the case?"

"Orders from above. Earnest's computer hard drives have been wiped clean. We've got almost nothing to work with."

The air went out of me. Earnest's hard drives had been wiped? The information on his computer was key to cracking the case. It had to be. It was the one place he could've interacted with his murderer. Which must be why the murderer destroyed it.

"How did it get wiped?" I asked. Not that the how of it mattered. We had about one in a million odds of even starting to solve the case now.

"The research team came a few minutes after you left yesterday and picked up his computer equipment. All the data was gone when they got there. They've been trying to recover some information from it, but whoever did the erasure knew what they were doing."

I remembered what Humphrey had said about Earnest leaving alone. And the video footage of him purchasing Cheetos Bolitas. Also alone. "It couldn't have been Earnest, could it?"

"I was hoping you could tell me," Connor said. "That's why you're back on the case."

I rubbed my face and thought about it. "Wait, do you mean it was completely erased? Like, all the settings and everything?"

"Yes."

"Then it wasn't Earnest."

"How do you know?"

"Because when I was looking for him yesterday morning,

I went to his computer desk, and his custom screensaver was on. It's a compilation of all his favorite space vessels. No way is that a default setting." Conviction and anger stirred in my belly. Earnest hadn't done this to himself. Someone had done this to him.

"If you're right, it means someone snuck into his apartment and erased the hard drives after you went looking for him at eight thirty and before we came back at eleven."

"I know," I said, my brain whirring over the implications. It explained why the mouse was half off its pad too. "And I'm right. I'm sure of it."

6

LOSING EARNEST'S COMPUTER data was a major blow. Next, I'd find out we had to solve the case blindfolded with our legs tied together.

The main problem with that was I wouldn't be able to concentrate on anything but Connor's leg pressed against mine.

"What *do* we have to go on then?" I asked.

"Phone records." Connor handed me a bunch of papers. "And your powers of recall."

Oh boy. I skimmed the lines of phone numbers and time stamps and wished again for spy training. Plus I wouldn't mind one of those pens that shoot tranquilizer darts. Especially while Aunt Alice was in town.

I clutched the papers without examining them more closely. What if I did and couldn't think of anything? I didn't want to squash our hopes of finding Earnest's killer. "What else do we have? What about the big whistle-blowing project he was working on for his website? Isn't that why he hired me?"

"Do you know who he was looking into?"

"No, he didn't like talking about it until he had all his ducks in a row."

"Well he didn't tell us either. He wrote down his website BusiLeaks as the reason he needed protection, without getting any more specific. We have all his past stories of course, but the repercussions for the people and companies he's already ousted have come and gone. Revenge is a possible motive, but not as good a motive as stopping your secrets being spilled in the first place."

That was bad. It never occurred to me he wouldn't have at least told the Taste Society what he was working on.

Connor took a left hand turn. Until now I'd been assuming, without really thinking about it, that we were going to Earnest's apartment, but the last turn took us off course. "If we have no leads, where are we going?"

"To your psychologist appointment."

"What?" I may have shrieked a little.

"A source let me know that the LAPD are going to rule Earnest's death as a murder or homicide and open an investigation, but it'll be another half day or so before that's official."

It's what my instincts had told me all along, but hearing it still hurt. Someone had done this to him. Cut his life ruthlessly short.

"Until then, I can't call myself a police consultant, and for the sake of a handful of hours, I'd prefer to introduce myself to suspects as a consultant rather than a PI."

I remembered we were talking about my psychologist appointment.

"Sure, but—"

"The last person Earnest called at twelve forty-five a.m. was a psychologist by the name of Dr. Kelly. You figured this out and have booked an appointment with her, as Earnest's grieving girlfriend, to find out why."

"But—"

"You'll be wearing a wire, of course." He opened the glove box and handed me my old faithful ladies' watch. It was as close to spy equipment as I was going to get. "Eleven o'clock was the only time slot she had available. Why do you think I gave you such short notice?"

Since he'd already told me twice today that being a jerk came naturally to him, I took it as a rhetorical question.

Fifteen minutes later, I entered an old double-story brick house that had been converted into offices and knocked on the door that had Dr. Kelly spelled out in neat letters on the opaque glass. It swung open to reveal a smiling woman in her thirties with skin the color of a caramel Frappuccino, quarter-inch-long black hair, and flawless white teeth. She was much younger and more chic than I'd expected.

"Happy holidays, Ms. Avery, please, come in. Can I offer you a refreshment of some kind? Tea, coffee, soda, juice, or water?"

"No, thank you."

"Are you sure? It's important you feel comfortable in this session." Her voice was pitched to that effect, warm and soothing.

"Thanks, but I just had a coffee." Maybe that's why I was feeling jittery.

She guided me to a navy armchair and seated herself in the other one. Her red suit jacket contrasted pleasantly against the navy fabric. She clasped her hands in her lap. "Then how can I help you today?"

"I'm not here for psychiatric treatment," I began.

"Of course not," she reassured me. "I'm a psychologist, not a psychiatrist."

"Uh, right." I fiddled with my watch. "And also, I'm Earnest Dunst's girlfriend. Or was, I mean."

"Is something wrong? You seem very nervous."

I cleared my throat, nervously. "Earnest is dead. You're the last person he called before he died. I'm trying to find out why."

Dr. Kelly's face blanched. "Earnest is dead? How? What happened?"

"That's what I want to know. I was told it looks like a heroin overdose, but I can't think why Earnest would fall off the wagon, and the police haven't ruled out foul play yet." I realized I was answering her questions instead of the other way around. And that I shouldn't have mentioned the last part. Shrinks made me flustered. "Can you tell me why he called you?"

She looked down at the form I'd hastily filled out. "Isobel. Oh, I remember now, he did talk about you, but he called you Izzy."

It was my turn to blanch. "He talked about me? What did he tell you?"

She smiled. "Patient confidentiality, Ms. Avery. I'm sure you understand how important it is."

I forced myself back on track. "So he was a patient of yours?"

She leaned against the armrest and studied me. Perhaps wondering how much to reveal. Or psychoanalyzing me from the way I sat and dressed and fiddled.

I stilled my hands.

"He was. I guess it doesn't hurt to tell you. He was working on his agoraphobia with me."

"How come I didn't know? Or his mom?"

She smiled again. It was an eerily calm and controlled

smile. Probably supposed to put me at ease, but it seemed unnatural to me and had the opposite effect. Who had their life as well ordered as that smile conveyed? Except maybe Connor, but he almost never smiled. And when he did it added life to his eyes, not this serene blankness.

"Earnest was seeing me in secret," she said. "He told me he wanted to surprise his loved ones with his progress, and I think, underneath that, he was scared of disappointing you if he failed."

I blew out a breath. "Oh."

"He was doing well. That's why he called me Thursday night, or Friday morning if you prefer. At first all our appointments were over the phone, but he'd begun to take short trips out of the house by himself and was slowly increasing how far he could go. It's a technique called exposure therapy. I would meet him at his destination goal and help him through his relaxation exercises. Thursday night he even managed to go into a convenience store and purchase something. He was very excited about it." Her serenity faltered. "What a shame he passed away so soon after making such a breakthrough."

Like that was the one reason to grieve his death. I cleared my throat again to buy me some time while I gathered my thoughts. "Why take those excursions in the middle of the night?"

Her tranquil mask was back. "To keep our sessions secret, of course. He also felt it was easier with less people around.

Less variables. Less environmental factors he couldn't predict or control."

It made sense. "Do you often work with your patients at such odd times?"

She leaned toward me. "I'm very dedicated to my patients, Ms. Avery. If they need me to meet with them out of hours, I make myself available. There is a surcharge, of course, but Earnest didn't mind."

It all made perfect sense. It explained the mystery of how and why Earnest left the house by himself. Corroborated what Humphrey saw. It even gave a reason for the Cheetos purchase.

What it didn't do was give us any leads whatsoever on who might have killed Earnest. Unless Dr. Kelly had done it. But as much as I didn't like shrinks, I couldn't come up with a motive for her.

I thought about the questions my fictional detectives would ask. "What time did you finish Thursday night's session?"

"Our sessions usually go from about twelve forty-five to one forty-five, so it would've been around then."

"Where did you part ways? Did you walk him home?"

"No, I left him outside Diego's Convenience Store. He was feeling up to going alone, and he knew I wouldn't be far away if he changed his mind." The store Earnest had bought the Cheetos from.

"Did Earnest talk to you about anyone who might've been a threat to him?"

Dr. Kelly looked at me curiously. These weren't the normal questions a grieving girlfriend would ask.

"Sorry," she said, "but I've stretched the terms of my confidentiality agreement as much as I'm willing to."

Probably not what Connor wanted to hear, but in Dr. Kelly's shoes, I wouldn't tell me anything more either.

Connor would have to come back when he had the weight of the LAPD behind him. "Then thank you for your time. It's been helpful."

Her smile made another appearance. "My pleasure, Ms. Avery. But we have thirty minutes left. Perhaps you should share why I make you so uncomfortable, and I might be able to help you in other ways."

I shot to my feet. "Uh, I'm good. Thanks." We shook hands, and I bolted out of her office as fast as my legs would carry me.

CONNOR LOOKED SMUG when I climbed back into the SUV. "Don't like doctors, huh?"

Levi's face flashed in my mind. "Just not head doctors, I guess."

"What are you afraid they'll find out?"

It was a good question. Maybe that I was as much of a mess as I thought I was. I flipped between despair and hope when it came to myself and my future, but I liked to hold on to the hope part.

"Can we focus on the case, please?" I asked.

Connor's body jerked a smidgen before he managed to repress the reaction.

I hid my satisfaction. Guess it wasn't every day that oh-so-professional Connor needed reminding he had a job to do.

"Right," he said. "Assuming our psych is telling the truth, what do we know about the murderer?"

He'd done this on the last case we'd worked together. Asked me questions to walk me through it and force me to draw my own conclusions. I wasn't sure why he bothered, but I mulled it over. "Do we have a time of death?"

"Between one thirty and three a.m."

One forty-five and three if Dr. Kelly was to be believed. "Well, there's no sign of a break-in or struggle at his apartment, so it's likely the killer apprehended him on his way home—"

"Unless it was someone he trusted."

"Right." It was true, but I didn't like it. The list of names in that category was very short: Mrs. Dunst, Jay Massey, and me. "But the timing seems pretty coincidental if it has nothing to do with his psychology appointment."

Connor checked his blind spot and pulled out onto the road. "I'll give you that. But it doesn't rule out the people he trusted. If they learned about his psych appointments, they might have chosen the time and method to divert attention from themselves."

Great. Being murdered by someone you love was worse than being murdered by an associate. Even if it made no difference to the final outcome. But I couldn't believe Mrs. Dunst or Jay could be behind it. Mrs. Dunst fussed and worried over him as only a mother could, and the one time I'd ever seen Jay mad at him was when Earnest had skipped video calling in to his addiction support group meeting.

"What else?" Connor prompted.

"Well, the building where Earnest's body was left is almost two miles away from where he was supposed to be walking home. It's a long way to travel on foot, especially with an unwilling, anxious, or heavily drugged person, so he was probably transported in a vehicle at some point. Which means the murderer needed access to a car, as well as heroin or whatever killed him. Given how it was set up to look like an overdose, I'm betting they knew about Earnest's drug history. That's not surprising as he freely admits to it on BusiLeaks, but it all adds up to suggest that the murder was planned in advance."

"Good."

"The obvious motive I can see is revenge for an exposé on his blog, or as you said, to stop him ousting someone's secrets in the first place."

"What about money?"

"Well, I'm not sure if he would've left a will, but I'm guessing either way that most of it would go to his mom. There's no chance it was her. She loves Earnest with all her heart."

Connor looked less convinced. "You're so jaded," I told him.

"You're so naive."

Probably fair. My ex had done a real number on me, and I didn't want to repeat that experience. But I also didn't want to become a total hard-ass like Connor. Though he did have a particularly great hard ass.

"Did anybody else love Earnest?" he asked. "Enough to kill him?"

"You have a strange idea of love. Maybe you should've been the one to see the psych." I was still kind of upset he'd made me do that.

He raised one eyebrow far enough that I knew he was doing it for effect. "That's rich coming from you. I'm not the one who married a scumbag."

I crossed my arms over my chest. "I feel like I'm at a disadvantage with you knowing my history when I don't know anything about yours."

"Yes," he said. "Now answer my question about Earnest."

It took me a moment to remember what he'd asked. "I don't think so. I'm the closest thing he'd had to a girlfriend in at least two years." Earnest might've been the closest thing I'd had to a boyfriend in about the same. "Besides, he only interacted in real life with three people, including me. Four if you count Dr. Kelly. If anybody loved or hated him for reasons outside his website, they would've had to meet him online."

"Which is why his computer would've been extremely useful," Connor said. "Whoever wiped it deleted his emails as well. The tech team is trying to hunt down his online accounts and activity on any web forums. We'll have to see what they dig up. In the meantime, I want you to talk to his friend, Jay Massey."

"That could be a problem."

"Why?"

"He thought I was after Earnest for his money. He'll probably think I killed him."

7

I WALKED GRUDGINGLY up the steps to Jay's beach-bungalow-style unit, which was nowhere near the beach. It was in University Park, six blocks from Earnest's. Connor didn't care that Jay Massey hated my guts. Sure, he'd promised to come charging in if I was in physical danger, but he didn't understand that most non-cyborgs fear awkward emotional situations almost as much as bodily harm. Personally, I'd prefer another encounter with Meow's claws over Jay's barbed words.

Maybe Connor thought my talking to Jay would reveal something useful. Or maybe he had some time to kill before the LAPD opened the official case and figured he may as well be entertained. *Jerk.*

I reminded myself, as I always did before facing Jay, that it wasn't personal. That his hostility toward me came from his loyalty and love for his dearest friend, his urge to protect.

He'd had front-row seats to Earnest's rapid rise up the corporate ladder, his breakneck descent into anxiety, self-medication, addiction, and self-destruction, and his subsequent attempts to piece together a life for himself. As the sole friend who'd stuck by him, Jay had every right to be overprotective.

So he'd told me when he cornered me in the kitchen and threatened to hack my accounts and make my life hell if I did anything to hurt Earnest.

There'd been a gentle fragility about Earnest that had brought out the protective side in me too.

Fat lot of good that had done.

The doorbell made a harsh buzzing sound. I waited. Caught myself fiddling with the watch again—the one that was sending audio to Connor—and stopped so as not to draw attention to it. After a minute or two, I gave the doorbell another buzz. Nothing.

Either Jay had spied me coming and was ignoring me, or he wasn't home. Hard to tell when his unit had an enclosed garage. Unless he was missing as well. Logic said it wasn't likely, but my stomach responded by twisting tighter anyway.

My unease meant I was almost happy to see him when he opened the door.

His expression told me he didn't feel the same way. "What are you doing here?" His hands, face, and clothes were speckled with white paint, and the fumes coming from inside suggested it was wet. Must be why he took such a long time to answer. His eyes looked like they'd been outlined with red paint. I guessed he'd been crying. A lot.

"Can I come in?"

To my surprise, he shrugged with resignation. "Sure."

I'd never been to his house before. I followed him down a narrow hallway, made even more narrow by the stacks of moving boxes, and stared at the series of photos depicting a much younger Earnest and Jay in full costume at some kind of sci-fi convention. My favorite was the one where Earnest was dressed as Princess Leia and Jay as Zoe from *Firefly*. Jay looked surprisingly pretty as a black woman. I wondered what they'd used for the fake boobs.

We turned into a kitchen and dining area where the paint fumes were even stronger. Jay must have led me here on autopilot as I couldn't imagine he'd offer me a drink.

His decorating tastes were a far cry from the beach-bungalow theme promised by the exterior. The dining table was black and chrome, and while half of the facing wall had been painted white, it was going to take more than one coat to hide the blacks and blues underneath. I stepped closer. The whole wall had been a mural of space. "Did you paint this?"

"The white paint all over me should answer that for you."

I turned around to see his arms were crossed, uninviting. No hint of the wide grin in the photos.

"I meant the mural," I said.

His eyes informed me that he knew what I'd meant. Then his arms slipped apart and down to his sides, as if they were too heavy to hold up. "Yes."

"It's good," I told him honestly.

He slouched into a dining chair. The last time I'd seen him seated was on Earnest's couch, the pair of them cackling like hyenas on a sugar high as they blew each other to smithereens on the flat screen.

"The landlord didn't think so," he said. "She wants it gone before I move."

Earnest had told me Jay's online courses on YouTube marketing were becoming popular and he was moving to a nicer place in Culver City.

I sat down too. "I'm sorry about Earnest."

Moisture pooled in his eyes. "Dammit." He rubbed his sleeved forearm across his face like a toddler might, smudging the paint there. "I can't believe he's dead. He'd been clean for fifteen months. Fifteen months! And we were chatting online Thursday—it must have only been hours before he died—and he was cheerful as could be." He looked at me with suspicion. "Did you two fight?"

"No. He was happy and normal when I left him Thursday night as well. I don't understand it."

"Right." He wiped his face again. "Right."

I waited while he gathered himself.

"Mrs. D. said you found him."

I nodded and pushed away the memory of it. "I did."

"Are they sure it's an overdose? Did it look like one?"

I swallowed the lump in my throat. Why was he asking? Because he didn't believe his best friend had killed himself, or because he wanted to make sure the police did? "I guess. I didn't . . . I mean I couldn't bear to get too close. I think they're doing an autopsy to make sure."

Something flickered across Jay's face. Worry? Anger?

"Do you think something else might have killed him?" I asked.

"Shit. I don't know." His shoulders slumped even lower, and he frowned at the table. "I don't even know what's worse."

"Do you—"

Jay stood up and gestured angrily at the wall. "I need to finish this coat so the paint has time to dry. Thanks for dropping by." In case I didn't know a dismissal when I heard one, he added, "You can let yourself out."

I was in the process of doing that when he called out

again. "And if you're hoping you'll get something in his will, you won't!"

I took a deep breath and told myself all the reasons I should ignore it. He was grieving. It wasn't personal. He was trying to protect—screw it. I stormed back into the dining room. "Listen, you moron, I never wanted his money! I hope Mrs. Dunst gets it all. You call yourself his best friend, but you're a blind idiot for not seeing how much Earnest had to offer a girl besides his bank balance. So back the hell off!"

Then I let myself out.

FEELING SHEEPISH, I gave my visual report to Connor. He'd already heard the audio version, but he didn't mention my outburst, despite the possibility that his ears were still ringing from the sudden decibel shift. Tactful. Not an attribute I associated with Connor. Maybe he thought I'd yell at him too.

We headed to a Korean hole-in-the-wall restaurant to refuel while we went through the phone records. It had the typical dingy tables and chairs and the usual delicious smells. Nice to know not everything needed a facelift to survive in LA where beauty was placed on a pedestal above every other virtue.

I was feeling virtuous about my meager banana and coffee for breakfast, so I ordered the crispy pork belly. Then I remembered that damn button.

Had it not been for Connor watching on, I might've changed my order to a salad, but I didn't want to draw his attention to my weight gain.

Plus after facing the shrink and then Jay, I really wanted the crispy pork belly.

Connor chose the duck curry before turning to scrutinize me. "I get the idea you were fond of Earnest. Were you two—"

"No. But I liked him a lot. He made a much nicer fake boyfriend than you did."

Connor's lip twitched. The equivalent of Oliver's grin. "I'm not surprised." His eyes fell to where I was tearing my napkin into thin strips. "How are you holding up?"

I forced myself to put the rest of the napkin down, unmolested. "Honestly?"

"Honestly."

It was something I'd been avoiding thinking about. But maybe I needed to talk about it. To process my feelings, just a little. So I didn't yell at any more of our leads. "Earnest was . . . smart, kind, and a lot of fun in his socially awkward way. He might've been scared to go outside, but he was trying to make the world better. I'm . . . angry, as you may have noticed. I want to get justice for him."

Connor's expression was gentle when I looked at him again. "Do you need me to take you to a shooting range?"

He'd done that for me when the last case had gotten overwhelming. I remembered the feel of his body pressed against my back. Solid. Strong. Seductive. "No," I said, heading off my thoughts and the rush of warmth in my stomach, "but thanks for offering."

He laid out the telephone records on the table, lightly brushing my hand as he did so. "Then let's find the bastard who did this."

It wasn't as hard to work out as I thought it might be. Most of the numbers were the same four. Mrs. Dunst's, Jay Massey's, Dr. Kelly's, and mine. I focused on the few that weren't, staring at the beginning and end times of the calls, trying to think back.

I pointed to the most recent unknown number, on Thursday night. "That one was a telemarketer I think. We were eating dinner, and Earnest told whoever it was that he wasn't interested and to take him off their list." I briefly entertained the thought that the telemarketer might have done it. I'd met a telemarketer-turned-hitman once, but his couldn't be the normal career progression.

My finger hovered over the next unknown number. "That might have been the landlord, calling about when someone could come and look at the water pressure problem. You can double check that, right? They've had a string of bad luck with building maintenance lately, so there'll be others to the same number."

"Should be easy enough to confirm."

I was coming up to phone calls from four days ago, and my memories were getting more and more hazy. One sparked a memory. "That one. Can you trace the number to find out who it is? We were binge watching the last few episodes of *Firefly*, and Earnest paused it to take the call in another room. I overheard some of the conversation."

Connor lifted an eyebrow in his understated way.

"What? I wasn't eavesdropping. The walls are thin. Earnest said something like, 'Sure I can meet with you, but you aren't going to change my mind. People need to know.' I assumed he was talking about his latest whistle-blowing project."

Connor sent a text. "Good. We should know who that number is registered to shortly."

A tinny version of "Girls Just Want to Have Fun" rang out on my phone. Oliver had changed it one night, trying to convince me to go out drinking with him. I rummaged through my bag for it, ignoring Connor's probable amusement. Unknown caller. "Hello?"

"I was expecting to see you down at the station yesterday, Ms. Avery." It was Commander Hunt.

"Um—"

"Get down here. Now." The growl in his voice would've sent Dudley cowering behind the couch. He disconnected before I could respond. Ugh. Why did everyone keep doing that to me? Jim, Connor, and now Hunt. They'd get along great if they could put aside their tough male egos and realize how much they had in common.

Connor was waiting for an explanation.

"That was Commander Hunt. He'd like me to come in and give my statement."

"He must have heard the coroner will be declaring the death as murder or homicide and wants to get a surreptitious start while the last paperwork is filed." He looked me over. "It might be best if you drive yourself. The less you have to do with me, the better as far as your relationship with Commander Hunt is concerned."

I tried not to feel abandoned as we headed back to Palms, but I suspected I was being offered up as a distraction while Connor raced to one-up Hunt.

"How much am I allowed to tell him?" I asked. I didn't relish the idea of lying to him. Or even worse, the idea of him catching me lying to him.

"Everything pertinent to the case," Connor said.

I loosed a breath in relief.

"He knows about Shades and their clients, so you can be open about that. You better tell him what you've learned today too. We're cooperating, remember?"

"Yes," I said, opening my car door. "That must be why you don't even want to be seen dropping me at the station."

Connor caught hold of my arm and waited until I looked back at him. "Don't be afraid of Hunt. He uses fear like it's going out of fashion. Which it is as far as LAPD public relations is concerned. You'll do fine."

He let go, and I slipped out of the cocoon of the SUV, not feeling any better.

Easy for him to say. I was twenty-nine years old and still scared of my aunt.

8

THE 27TH STREET COMMUNITY Police Station was an old double-story gray brick building that, like Hunt, had so far escaped the LAPD's efforts to improve public trust by changing the face of law enforcement to a more friendly and approachable one.

I parked in the lot and made extra sure I was neatly between the white lines before heading in. The uninviting, gray theme continued inside with easy-to-clean tiles and unnecessarily low ceilings strewn with cheap tinsel. I approached the kind-looking officer behind the front counter and yelped when Hunt materialized at my side. "Follow me."

He led me past a bunch of uniforms hunched over desks, most of them too busy to spare me a glance, but one offered a smile. Even so, I squelched down the memory of the stop sign I accidentally ran that time in case any of them had mind reading powers.

Logically, being surrounded by police should've made me feel safe, but for some reason I always felt nervous and guilty instead. I wasn't sure what that said about me. Dr. Kelly would've had a few ideas.

I attempted to find comfort in the hum of noise. Telephones ringing. Keyboards clacking. The rise and fall of a dozen conversations. If I shut my eyes, it could've been any open office space. Of course, if I'd shut my eyes, I might also run into Hunt's unforgiving back.

We entered the interrogation room, and any fancies I had of being elsewhere dissipated. It was like you see on TV, only smaller. A bare, windowless room with one-way glass and a table and chairs bolted to the floor.

Commander Hunt's blue eyes harpooned me to my uncomfortable seat, and I gathered that he wouldn't be the one to change my anxiety issues with law enforcement.

If we had been back in the Old West, he would've had me lassoed, lying in the dust with his foot on my chest. If we'd been deep inside a war zone, he would've been roughing me up, waving a weapon in my face, threatening torture. But we were in the twenty-first century in Los Angeles, California, so he offered me coffee.

Based on the whiff I'd had of the sludge as I'd walked

through the office, drinking it might be considered a form of torture, so I shook my head. "No thanks."

Muttering something about editing out Taste Society references before putting it on file, Hunt switched on the microphone. Trusting this was the agreement, I identified myself for the recording. Connor had told me to tell him everything.

"What was the nature of your relationship with Earnest Dunst?"

"According to public knowledge, he was my boyfriend, but that was a cover. He hired me to protect him against poison attempts."

"And now give me an answer I can leave on the tape."

"He was my boyfriend."

We went over the basics like this. How long I'd known him. What we did together. The day leading up to his death. What time I left Thursday evening. When I noticed he was missing. How I came to find his body. And on and on it continued. The same questions asked in different ways. To catch me out if I was lying. Lucky I wasn't lying.

"How did you feel about him?"

I had no desire to start crying in front of Hunt, so I kept it light. "I guess I thought of him like a kid brother. I enjoyed his intelligence and humor, laughed at his nerdiness, and occasionally wanted to beat some sense into him."

"Where were you between one thirty and three a.m.?"

Oh no. "The beating thing was just a figure of speech."

"Answer the question, Avery." The growl in his voice had returned. I wondered if he'd ever consider doing voice-over for a werewolf movie.

"I was home. Sleeping."

"Can anyone vouch for that?"

Oliver had been at work. I chewed my lip. "That depends. Can I call a cat to the witness stand?"

He scowled at me.

"Or a nosy neighbor? A very observant one who always knows what's going on in the building?"

"Not unless she was sleeping with you."

"Ah, that would be a no then."

"Do you have any other knowledge that might be pertinent to this case?"

I outlined what Connor and I had learned in the past two days. As I spoke, Hunt's jaw got tighter and tighter, and the growl in his voice grew more and more pronounced. I assumed he was pissed that Connor had such a lead on him until he switched off the recorder and leaned so far across the table that his prickly mustache threatened to stab me in the nose.

"Listen carefully, Avery, because I'm only going to tell you once. You will cease all attempts to learn more about this case immediately. Understaffing and underfunding means I don't have a choice about working with Stiles as a consultant, but I will not"—his finger ground into the table like it was a particularly noxious cigarette—"have a *civilian* interfering with this investigation. Do you understand?"

I gave a weak nod. Did he mean *suspect* when he said civilian? In the movies the cops were always suspicious of the victim's significant other and the person who discovered the body. I was both.

"That was a question," he barked.

"Yes, I understand, Commander."

"Good. Because I'd hate to toss your ass in jail for obstruction of justice over a misunderstanding."

I would bet my last pair of clean socks that he'd love to toss my ass in jail. For any reason. "Yes, Commander."

He withdrew a fraction, his point made. "One more thing."

"Yes?"

"Don't leave town."

So much for not being afraid.

IT WAS DARK when I trudged back to my carefully parked Corvette, and I decided I'd had enough for one day. Connor could wait. Mrs. Dunst could wait. Thinking about Commander Hunt's warnings could wait. I drove home to lick my metaphorical wounds and take antibiotics for my physical ones.

Connor texted me to say the phone number I'd pointed out was a burner, paid for in cash in a store without surveillance. In other words, a dead end. No new leads from the research team digging into Earnest's online accounts either.

He also asked how giving my statement went, but I couldn't summon the energy to respond. Tomorrow would be soon enough to tell him we wouldn't be working together anymore.

I lay down on my horrible duvet cover, which looked like a rainbow Paddle Pop ice cream had vomited and used the fabric to mop it up. It was secondhand, like everything else in my bedroom, except for the new sheets I'd sprung for when I'd first moved in. The wardrobe was blue, the bedside table yellow, and the carpet the same musty old green as the rest of the apartment. Even the lampshade was an orange, tasseled eyesore that had probably been here when the place was built fifty odd years ago. Nevertheless, with a book in my hand and Meow curled up on my belly, her black paint-dipped paw twitching in sleep, I didn't care about any of it.

I devoured another six chapters of David Sedaris's collection of essays but still didn't want to face anything important, so I made good on my end of the deal with Oliver by cleaning the apartment. Two hours later, I was putting the last of my clothes into my wardrobe and realizing that between poverty, weight gain, and the change of season in LA, I had very little to wear until it got warm again. Nor any black and formal outfits for Earnest's funeral.

Between the clothes and my room, it might be a good thing I was once again booted off the investigation to allow me to go shopping. I'd received two paychecks since earning out the advance, so I had some spending money. But I was ever mindful that with the ridiculous fifteen percent interest rate, every dollar I spent now cost me a lot more in the life of the loan.

I slumped against my wardrobe. I hated shopping. Especially clothes shopping. Wading for hours through the sea of people and fabric to the beat of loud, obnoxious music trying to find something that was comfy, affordable, and made me look okay—all for the sake of a basic necessity was exhausting for me. And Christmas was the worst possible time to go, with throngs of frantic, pushy shoppers, Mariah Carey crooning about her Christmas wish ad nauseam, and exhausted retail staff ready to stuff their ears with styrofoam snow just to keep from screaming.

How anyone preferred shopping over reading in bed with a cat for company was beyond my understanding.

Oliver rescued me from considering whether this was how crazy-cat-lady syndrome starts by charging through the front door and into my bedroom.

"Izzy, I think I'm in love." To illustrate the drama of the situation, he belly flopped onto my bed and then soothed an indignant Meow, who had been curled up peacefully on my rainbow-vomit pillow.

I knew he'd been attracted to Henrietta, and I'd shamelessly leveraged the fact, but I hadn't seen this coming. I'd assumed that after a whole day in her company, he'd have looked beyond the pretty exterior to the devil within.

"I'm sorry to hear that," I said gravely.

"She's poised, beautiful, and so self-possessed! Not a hair out of place. Even those hard-nosed business types go out of their way to let her past on the sidewalk. How can I not admire that?"

"Sounds like Her Majesty the Queen."

Oliver loved to rant about his monarch and was appalled and flabbergasted that so many admired her. I found his rants entertaining, so I poked fun at him whenever I could.

He shot me a withering look. "There's nothing admirable about getting special treatment because you were conceived in the right bed. Did you know that thanks to a preposterous statute passed by King Edward II in the fourteenth century, she technically owns all the whales, dolphins, porpoises, and sturgeons within three miles of the UK? I mean, can you imagine waving your hand and saying, 'Oh yeah, I own all those swimmy sea creatures now?' Of course hard-nosed business types would get out of her way, otherwise she might take possession of their businesses!"

"I'm not sure people would stand for that in the twenty-first century."

"Oh the monarchy might not be so obvious about it, but they'd make it happen. You can't trust royalty. But Henrietta's strong without the self-entitlement part. And she's not all dramatic and emotional like Adele was. Henrietta would never want to become an actress." Adele was the girl Oliver had come to Los Angeles for.

"That's probably true, but—"

"I think I'm winning her over too, but it's hard with Mrs. Sloan chaperoning us." Mrs. Sloan was Aunt Alice. "You have to invite her to do something with you tomorrow so I can get some alone time with Henrietta."

I got to my feet. "Invite the woman I described to you earlier today as my worst nightmare to do something with me? The one I agreed to cook anything you wanted and clean the apartment for two whole weeks to avoid?"

He rolled over and looked at me, eyes pleading. "Pleeeeeease."

I felt my shoulders drop and knew I was defeated even before I opened my mouth. "Fine. I'll think of something to keep her busy for a few hours. But you realize Aunt Alice would become your mother-in-law right?"

He got up, threw his arms around me, and planted a loud kiss on my cheek. "And you'd be my cousin-in-law! Thanks, Iz, you're the best."

9

AT NINE O'CLOCK the next morning, I sat on Mrs. Dunst's plump orange couch opposite Jay. All traces of paint were gone, but his eyes were still red and his arms still too heavy. He was glaring at me, but in an empty kind of way that made me think it was out of habit more than anything else. Like how, even now, a part of me hoped to please Aunt Alice despite knowing it was impossible.

My eyes were red too. I'd performed my morning routine with encouragement from Earnest's app and then bawled all the way here. I'd finally switched the app off after that.

Mrs. Dunst bustled between us, pouring a soda for Jay and a tea for herself and me. It was a scene I was familiar with, though it had always taken place at Earnest's previously. If it weren't for the location and the fact he wasn't here, I might've been able to pretend nothing worse had happened but an aggressive strain of pinkeye.

She settled into her own overstuffed floral armchair, next to the Christmas tree that was adorned with twinkle lights, baubles, and a handful of colorful, misshapen decorations that Earnest must have made when he was a child. My throat started aching again.

"Thank you both for coming," she said. "I have some news about Earnest. The police wanted me to keep it to myself until tomorrow, but—"

"Are you sure you shouldn't do what the police said?" I asked, realizing what she was about to say. It was very unlikely Jay had done it, but if he had, it would ruin the element of surprise when Connor or Commander Hunt questioned him. An element of surprise that might give them vital information.

"I don't see what harm it could do, and you both deserve to know given you loved him too."

Crap.

"The police think Earnest was"—her teacup trembled violently—"murdered."

Jay Massey looked like he'd been slapped. I tried to appear equally shocked, but it didn't matter because Mrs. Dunst wasn't looking at us anyway.

She lifted the cup toward her lips but thought better of it when some of its contents slopped over the rim. Her hands lowered again, resting the cup back in her lap. "They said it was a heroin overdose, like we already believed. But that someone else injected it. That there were signs of a . . . struggle and the angle of the needle was wrong."

I would've taken the cup from her, except I suspected the ongoing challenge of hanging on to it might be all that was keeping her from falling apart.

"They're opening an investigation and told me they'd do everything possible to find who did this. But I thought . . ." She let out a shaky breath. "I thought you deserved to know."

At last she lifted her gaze.

My heart lurched in sympathy. "Oh, Mrs. Dunst—"

"No! He can't have been." Jay shot to his feet, slopping soda over his hand, but he didn't notice. "Who was behind it? I'll kill the bastard."

"That's nice of you to say, darling," Mrs. Dunst said. She called everyone darling. "But it won't bring Earnest back, and he wouldn't like to see you in prison."

Jay deflated.

"Anyway, I'm sure the police will have questions for you both, but I didn't want them to spring the news on you. If they find out you were here this morning, you can say I asked you to come and talk about the funeral."

Jay stalked out soon afterward. He was under the pump to get everything packed in time for the moving van.

I lingered behind. "Can I help with anything?"

She smiled a sad smile. "That's so sweet of you. They're releasing his . . . him today, and I have to start funeral planning, but how can I? How can I plan to bury my beautiful boy?"

I took her hand, trying not to look at the Christmas tree. "I don't know."

"I keep thinking that I should've stopped it somehow. Should've found him quicker. Shouldn't have doubted him."

"Don't. He was lucky to have you, and he knew it. You're a great mother." It was true. She was a lot like her couches. Plump and not particularly fashionable, but snug and welcoming and good in a way that beat the sleek, pretentious variety without contest.

She squeezed my hand until it hurt and blinked tears from her eyes. "Do you think Jay will be okay?"

I recognized the tactic. Focus on a lesser problem to avoid the hairy mammoth standing in your living room. I'd been employing it solidly for the past two days.

"He took it pretty hard," she went on, "and he was already feeling guilty. I should've told him it didn't matter, that it wouldn't have mattered."

"What wouldn't?" I asked.

She retrieved the tissues from her pocket and wiped her

cheeks. "Jay felt bad for not helping us search. He was in the middle of painting something for the landlord, and we agreed he should finish it and join us afterward, but by then . . . And it wouldn't have helped, you know? Earnest was . . . gone before we even started looking."

"I don't think any of us could've done anything." I meant it, yet as I said the words, I wondered if they were true for me. Had I missed something? I'd spent every day with him for months. There must have been some kind of warning that he was in danger.

She wiped her eyes again. "You're right, of course. And regrets won't bring him back either." She blew her nose and then, finally, took her first sip of tea.

It would have been lukewarm at best. Kind of like Connor's feelings about seeing me again.

She squared her shoulders and looked up at me. "I've been trying to think about his funeral. I know which funeral home I want to use, but I haven't been able to bring myself to make an appointment. Do you think . . . Would you mind going with me?"

I'd rather stick a fork in my eye. "Of course not," I said.

AFTER WE'D FINISHED wading through the exhausting number of options with the funeral home, I caught myself driving on autopilot to Earnest's apartment. I still didn't know what to do about Commander Hunt's ultimatum, and it seemed as good a place to think it over as any. Besides, my muffins were going to waste.

Connor had tried to call me twice, but I'd let it go to voice mail. I wasn't ready to relay what had happened with Hunt yet. Or discuss what it meant for our investigation.

I kept thinking about those erased hard drives. It made the whole case damn near impossible, so logic suggested the killer was behind it. Which added weight to the idea that Earnest was murdered to stop him publishing his most recent exposé, but one thing didn't make sense to me. If Earnest was killed between one forty-five and three a.m. and the hard drives wiped much later between eight thirty and eleven, what happened in the intervening hours?

Surely it didn't take that long to remove incriminating evidence? So why had the killer waited until then, when there was more chance of being discovered? Was it possible the murder and the data deletion were performed by different people? Except they had to be linked. It was too coincidental to make sense otherwise.

It seemed that despite Hunt's demands, my mind, at least, was on the case.

As I secured a parking spot for my Corvette, I wondered if the police might be in Earnest's apartment. Unlikely since the Taste Society's team had already swept the place, and with confirmation that Earnest left of his own accord, it wasn't a crime scene.

There was no telltale police tape on the door, so I let myself in. The place was a mess. Apparently the Taste Society forensic and investigation team took less care when the owner was dead. I suppose dead people don't complain. Even so, it made me cringe on Earnest's behalf. If he'd been here to see it, the upheaval of all his ordered belongings would've greatly upset him.

I straightened two of the skewed posters and propped the umbrella up in its corner before I stopped myself. It wouldn't bring Earnest back. It might get my ass thrown in jail.

Ugh. What was I doing here? I should leave. But not without my muffins.

Mind made up, my feet retraced the path I'd taken so many times toward the kitchen. Except this time, a breeze tickled my skin. I halted midstride. Had the Taste Society team left a window ajar? I followed the breeze into Earnest's bedroom to close it, but the window wasn't ajar.

It was smashed.

I grabbed my phone and was debating whether to call Connor, Commander Hunt, or the landlord first when Earnest's wardrobe door flew open. It rammed into me with the force of a champion sumo wrestler, and I hit the floor hard enough to make my teeth rattle. Shocked, I took an instant to move. A shadow fell over me. Pain blossomed in the back of my head, and darkness swallowed me whole.

Seconds later, light rushed in and I heard footsteps on the pavement outside. Hurrying away.

I sat up fast, thinking to get a glimpse of the person, but a wave of dizziness sent me face-first back onto the floor. I waited for the vertigo to subside, then eased myself gingerly into a sitting position.

The new vantage point accentuated the pain bouncing around my skull, and since the footsteps were long gone and there was no one around to hear me, I took the liberty of whimpering.

My phone was lying on the carpet nearby where I'd dropped it as I fell. I picked it up and groaned again. Me and my new nine pounds must have landed on it. The screen was cracked. I tapped the fractured glass and was relieved when it lit up under my fingertips. I dialed Connor. For some reason I always defaulted to calling him in the face or aftermath of danger.

"Nice of you to decide to talk to me," he said in his usual dry tone.

"Earnest's apartment has been ransacked, and—"

"Get out now. The intruder could still be there."

Definitely should have called him earlier.

"Too late. I assumed the mess was from the forensic and investigation team until someone knocked me on the head."

Connor said a naughty word. "Are you okay?"

"I think so, except for a mean headache anyway. Unfortunately, I didn't see the person responsible for it."

"Stay where you are. I'm on my way."

My throbbing skull convinced me to follow his advice. While I waited, I wondered who might've been going through Earnest's apartment when the computer had already been wiped. Was it an opportunist stealing stuff? It made a sick kind of sense to rob the recently deceased. I looked around, but the $380 Kindle Oasis sitting in plain sight on his bookshelf didn't support the theory.

Could it have been the killer removing some type of obscure evidence he'd forgotten about until now? I shivered. Somehow being brained by Earnest's murderer was a lot creepier than being brained by a random thug.

Long minutes later, I tensed at the sound of the front door opening. Not that it made any sense for the intruder to come back through the front door even if they had decided to finish the job.

"Isobel?"

My heart sped up until I placed the voice. Levi. Then it beat faster for a different reason. It had been less than forty-eight hours from when I'd turned him down, and while he'd taken it well, I hadn't expected to see him again so soon. I still wasn't sure I'd made the right decision.

"In here," I called, cursing Connor for reporting the incident.

Levi swept into the room like a breath of sunshine and cinnamon. "You know, I really was joking about being disappointed by your lack of being shot or poisoned lately," he said as he knelt down to examine me. "And there are easier ways to see me than getting knocked on the head. Like saying yes, next time I ask you out, for example." He shone a penlight in my eyes.

"Great tip," I mumbled.

"How are you feeling?" Gentle fingers probed the lump on my head.

"Okay."

"Liar."

"Well, okay for someone who's been hit on the head."

"Any vision impairment? Nausea?"

"No. But I wouldn't mind some pain relief."

He rocked back onto his feet and smiled at me. "Whatever the lady wants."

"I bet it's not often you get turned down," Connor said, startling both of us.

Levi recovered quickly. "Less often than you. I've heard your bedside manner is terrible."

Connor smirked. Then his eyes landed on me and the

smirk disappeared. "Are you sure she's okay?"

"Yes. But she shouldn't drive for twenty-four hours and will need monitoring overnight for concussion."

"I'll keep an eye on her. Save her going into the medical facility."

Maybe the head injury was more serious than Levi thought. I could've sworn Connor just volunteered to spend time with me.

I tried to read him to work out why, but his eyes had left me to scour the room, assessing every detail.

Levi rummaged through his kit and handed me a packet of pills along with a bottle of water to swallow them with. "Take two of these up to four times daily for the next couple of days until you're feeling better. And don't tell Connor since it's against Taste Society regs, but I'm giving you my business card again with my direct number on it." He winked at me. "Only because you can't seem to stay out of trouble, of course."

"I'll pretend I didn't hear that," Connor said, "since I think it's a good idea."

I busied myself by taking the pills and hoped the bottle of water would hide my face. The problem was, the plastic and liquid were both transparent, so it wasn't as effective as I would've liked. "Thank you both for the vote of confidence."

"We have every confidence in your ability to find trouble," Levi told me. "Call me when you do." He gathered his things and swept back out of the room, leaving me wondering again why I'd turned him down.

Connor's eyes rested on me for a few seconds before he spoke again. "Are you feeling up to standing?"

"Yes." I got up to prove it.

"Either this break-in was by a different person than whoever erased the hard drives, or they've grown careless now that Earnest's death has been ruled a murder. Can you take a look around to see if anything's missing?"

I walked through the five tiny rooms, being careful about where I placed my feet to avoid stepping on anything. "It's hard to tell when it's in this state, but I don't think anything's been taken," I concluded. "Except for the computers and hard drives, which I'm assuming the Taste Society team laid claim to."

Connor pulled out his phone. "That doesn't give us any clues about the intruder's identity or purpose then. We'll have to hope the crime scene unit finds something that does."

"The LAPD crime scene unit?"

"Yes."

I rubbed my nose where Hunt's mustache had almost stabbed it. This was bad. Really bad. "Any way you can avoid telling Commander Hunt I was here?"

Maybe Connor heard the edge of hysteria in my voice because he looked up from his phone and gave my question some thought before answering. "No. Not after the intruder attacked you. It could be important to the case, and your DNA might be found mixed up with theirs."

I let out a wobbly sigh. Would a Christmas miracle be too much to ask for?

Of course it would.

In lieu of a miracle, my mind turned to muffins. My headache was fading, Commander Hunt was looming, and I needed comfort food. "Would it count as tampering with a crime scene if I took my muffins home with me?"

Connor's lips twitched. "Now that I ought to be able to avoid telling Commander Hunt about."

I had an urge to hug him. But as amusing as his reaction might be, annoying him wasn't the best way to return his kindness.

He called to report the break-in to the police, and I phoned the landlord to fix the window. We went outside and found a patch of sunlight to wait in. I offered Connor a muffin, which he declined, and I bit into the white-chocolate-and-raspberry goodness myself. It would have been even better with a cup of tea, but I suspected that would be pushing the tampering thing.

"Is Hunt likely to come here?" I asked.

Connor eyed me. "Probably. What's up?"

Lucky the muffin was moist, or I'd have had a hard time swallowing. "I've been told in no uncertain terms that I need to stay out of the case, or he'll throw my ass in jail. I only came here to collect my muffins. The problem is, I'm not sure he'll believe me."

10

I WAS MORE FAMILIAR with Earnest's landlord than I should've been after a few months of working with Earnest. Mr. Bradley was a small mole of a man, with dark hair, dark eyes, and a mood to match. He even waddled rather than walked. I waved him over when he arrived.

"Don't take this the wrong way," he said, "but I was hoping not to have to see you again for at least another six months. This damn building is burning a hole in my pocket faster than my husband is, and that's saying something."

"Uh," I said.

"Who's this anyway?" he asked, squinting at Connor.

"I'm Connor Stiles, a consultant with the LAPD."

Mr. Bradley sucked in his cheeks. "Oh boy this can't be good. I hope you're not about to tell me my best tenant is in some kind of trouble."

"What makes you think he might be?" Connor asked.

Mr. Bradley's shoulders slumped. "Because that's the type of luck I'm having lately." He pointed at the building behind us. "I got four tenants in there. The place is rent controlled, and three of the four have been there for over a decade. Hell, one of them's been there two decades. That means they ain't paying nearly what they should be, and with the screwy wiring and hot water pressure issues of late, the rent's not even covering my costs. Mr. Dunst is the only one paying a fair price, so with a police consultant here and the broken window Ms. Avery reported, I'm betting it's not good news."

"I'm afraid you're correct," Connor said. "Mr. Dunst has been murdered."

Shock and horror flitted across Mr. Bradley's face. "No. I don't believe it." He reached up and removed his black fedora-style hat, wringing it in his hands with a desperate, single-minded focus. As if he could just find the right hidden lever, it would transform into a magic carpet and fly him away.

After about thirty seconds of this, his whole body sagged. "Oh no. Not in the apartment. No one'll want to rent it now." He was muttering to himself, oblivious to how he might be affecting Earnest's bereaved girlfriend. I was glad Mrs. Dunst wasn't the one breaking the news.

"The murder did not take place in the apartment, Mr. Bradley," Connor said. "But I suggest you rein in your thoughts and feelings on the matter." He made obvious eyes at me, and the landlord looked chagrined.

"Ah, I'm sorry, Ms. Avery. Sorry for your loss. Um. I guess you better show me that window."

A couple of uniformed policemen arrived shortly afterward, and between them, Mr. Bradley, Connor, and me, Earnest's tiny, ransacked bedroom felt more than a little crowded. Still, I counted my blessings. It wasn't nearly as claustrophobic as it might have been if Commander Hunt was there as well.

I was making a break for some fresh, outside air when I spotted him striding across the road. Pulse quickening, I slammed the door and squeezed myself into the bedroom again. Maybe he'd overlook me if I was one of the crowd.

Yeah right.

Commander Hunt's cold blue eyes locked onto me as soon as he entered. "Ms. Avery. A word."

He marched out to the front garden, and I followed, trying not to drag my feet. The wintry, fresh air I'd been longing for was somehow hard to breathe.

"I thought we had an understanding," he drawled. "What the hell were you doing here?"

I pretended to be fascinated by a plastic bag being chased by the wind to avoid his gaze. "Collecting some personal things."

"What things?" He leaned in close, looming over me, and making his voice equally threatening. "In case I didn't make myself clear, I wasn't bullshitting when I warned you about interfering in my investigation."

Great. I'd have to tell him. "Just my muffins. I swear."

He leaned back.

"I brought them over Friday before I knew Earnest was missing and then forgot to take them home. I didn't want them to go to waste. And his apartment isn't a crime scene, so I wasn't interfering! At least it wasn't a crime scene until an hour ago when some intruder bashed me over the head . . ."

A glint came into his eye. I suspected he was thinking the whack might do me good. "Let me get this straight. You were assaulted and sustained a head injury over some muffins?"

"I guess so, yes."

"Well." He almost looked pleased for a moment. "I hope for your sake that they're damn good muffins."

"They—"

"Let me clarify something for you. If I find out you're lying to me, the head injury's going to seem like the highlight of your week by the time we're through."

My hand involuntarily went to the swelling on my skull. "Yes, Commander."

He turned his back on me and strolled lazily into the apartment. Connor came out a minute later. As if they were playing a good-and-evil tag team. "You're not in handcuffs, so I assume that went as well as it could have," he observed. "Are you doing okay?"

"You mean aside from being brained over some muffins?"

"Yes."

I rubbed a weary hand over my face. I'd spent hours today helping Mrs. Dunst plan Earnest's funeral and witnessed how his death had blown her entire world to pieces. Yet his death just meant money in the funeral director's pocket, money out of the landlord's, and most people would go on with their lives as if he never existed. I didn't want to be one of them. His life meant something, and he deserved more from me. Mrs. Dunst did too. I wanted to help find his killer.

Before I could try to express any of that, my phone vibrated. The text was from an unknown number.

Find and destroy Earnest's backup flash drive, or the next time we meet will go a lot worse for you.

I handed my phone to Connor. "I guess we know what the intruder was looking for now."

CONNOR PASSED the phone back to me. "That's two reasons for you to sleep at my house tonight. Do you know anything about a flash drive?"

I racked my brain. This was the kind of scenario where my personal knowledge of Earnest might help crack the case. But it turned out that I couldn't divine where Earnest would store a backup flash drive even if my life depended on it. Which it might do if that text message was anything to go by. So much for inside information.

Connor hid his disappointment well. But then he hid all his feelings well.

He jogged away to let Hunt know about the text message and my ignorance. I stared after his athletic figure and wondered why events so often conspired to leave me feeling incompetent around him. When he returned, he patted me on the shoulder. He seemed to be doing that a lot lately. "Don't worry. We'll talk to Jay Massey. Maybe he'll know about the flash drive."

"You mean *you'll* talk to him." My tone was bitter. "Remember the whole tossing-my-ass-in-jail thing? Commander Hunt wants me as far away from this case as I can get. At least as far as I can get without leaving LA, given he considers me a suspect."

Connor weighed me up before speaking. "Well, it's your decision. But there are ways we could work around that."

"What? How?"

"I can't guarantee you won't get caught," he warned, "but I could wear a wire to allow you to listen in on any interviews. The same way we did with Massey but in reverse. You can lend your insight to the case while staying out of sight. It would have been hard to come up with a reason for Earnest's girlfriend tagging along with a police consultant anyway, so that will protect your cover as well."

It sounded good. Except for the part where I might get caught. The fact Connor was warning me suggested I'd be on my own if I did. Out of the Taste Society's sphere of protective influence. In jail, with only Commander Hunt's mercy to rest my hope in.

That bit wasn't good. That bit was very bad.

But today had demonstrated to me that regardless of Hunt's threats, I wouldn't be able to stop thinking about the case until Earnest's killer was caught. Of course, thinking about it and acting on it were distinctly different things from the commander's point of view. "Won't you get in trouble, too, if Hunt finds out you're working with me?"

Connor's lips flatlined. "I can handle Hunt."

So, that was a yes then. "Why would you go to the trouble of including me?"

He lightly traced the edge of my jaw then snapped his hand down as if remembering we weren't fake girlfriend and boyfriend anymore. "You mean, aside from needing to supervise you for the next twenty-four hours anyway?"

"Yes."

"Because. You were . . . kind of . . . helpful on the Josh Summers case."

"*Kind of* helpful? I believe I recall being the one who identified the poisoner."

"And I recall being the one who stopped said poisoner from shooting you."

"Okay. I see your point, but—"

He shrugged. "Hunt doesn't scare me, and we need all the help we can get. The LAPD got a warrant for Dr. Kelly's files, and we went over them all this morning trying to find promising leads. Unfortunately, Dr. Kelly was far more interested in Earnest's past than the present and didn't talk much about his BusiLeaks projects at all."

"But what about—"

"I'll sweeten the deal with an espresso every morning."

"That's so conniving of you."

Or nice.

"Are you in or out?" he asked.

Unlike Connor, I was terrified of Commander Hunt. But my alternative was to pretend I didn't care and hang out with Aunt Alice while Oliver and Henrietta slobbered on each other. "I'm in."

"Good. Let's—"

"Oh no." I stared at my cracked phone, willing the numbers to change.

"What's wrong?"

"I'm late for my date with Aunt Alice."

Connor stopped me from jumping in the Corvette and flooring it to Downtown. "No driving, remember?"

"But I need to go right now!"

"Then I'll drive. Get in the SUV."

I got in.

"Where are we going?" he asked.

"The shooting range you took me to on Twelfth Street."

He hit the accelerator. "Are you sure that's the best choice for someone with a head injury?"

"The head injury wasn't something I factored in when I came up with the plan this morning."

I'd thought long and hard about what to do with Aunt Alice and chosen the shooting range because the earplugs and noise would ensure a bare minimum of actual conversation. Plus it had given me an excuse to invite Etta.

Connor's features made the subtle shift into his version of a frown. "I'll have to come and supervise then. Head injuries and firearms don't play well together."

"No need for you to waste your time. Etta will be there to show Aunt Alice the ropes, and I'll probably sit it out."

"Etta's your idea of a responsible weapons instructor? I'll definitely have to come in."

I crossed my arms but didn't argue his point.

Twenty minutes later, despite the lack of conversation, I was regretting my choice of activity. I hadn't reckoned on how terrifying an armed Aunt Alice would be.

She was holding a Glock, like Etta's. Etta didn't believe in starting with a sensible training gun. Etta believed in starting with a cool gun.

The pair of them were wearing matching grins too, and that was even scarier than the matching guns. I'd been expecting disapproval from Aunt Alice, not fiendish glee.

"You look good with a Glock," Etta told her. "I'll bet you're a natural."

"Well don't just stand there gawking, Isobel," Aunt Alice said when she noticed me staring at them, transfixed with fear. "Take a photo so I can put it on Facebook."

I did as I was told and tried to ignore Connor's inevitable amusement while Etta and Aunt Alice posed with their guns. I prayed the weapons weren't loaded yet and took a bunch of photos. It was likely to be the safest part of the evening, after all.

"Let us see," Aunt Alice demanded. I handed her the phone, and they tittered over themselves like budgies in front of a mirror. Except less cute and more frightening. Maybe mutant monster budgies in front of a mirror.

I gave up on the budgie analogy when I noticed the dangerous duo had their heads together and were whispering about something. My neck prickled in warning.

Thankfully, their furtive looks weren't directed my way.

"Connor," Etta said, her voice dripping with syrupy sweetness, "perhaps you could help Mrs. Sloan here into the proper shooting stance. It's been an awful long time since I was taught, and I don't want to steer her wrong."

I didn't buy it for a second. And as Connor stepped forward to guide my aunt into position, I realized what was going on. Aunt Alice wanted Connor's hands on her, and this was their devious way of achieving it.

"I need to go to the bathroom," I announced. I was nauseous and suspected it had nothing to do with the lemon-sized lump on the back of my skull. Connor was the only one who seemed to hear. He made questioning eyes at me, but I shook my head and followed the signs to the restroom.

Let them have their fun so long as I didn't have to watch.

I dawdled as much as I could without drawing undue attention to the health of my intestines, and when I returned, Connor was once again at a safe distance from Aunt Alice. Though, judging by the wild variation in her shots, there may be no such thing as a safe distance.

After she'd made it through a few rounds, she'd hit her paper target a sad total of three times. She'd hit Etta's target and the one to the other side of hers about twice that. All Etta's shots were in the bullseye so it wasn't hard to differentiate.

Aunt Alice's cheeks were flushed, but whether from excitement or embarrassment I couldn't tell. Maybe both. The last shot of the clip embedded itself in the safety polyurethane flooring, and she turned the gun around and peered down the barrel. Connor strode forward and took it from her. "Never point the gun at yourself or anyone else even if you're sure it's not loaded."

"I was trying to see if it's working properly."

He reloaded it and casually proceeded to shoot five shots into the middle ring, one-handed. He passed it back to her. "It's working properly—you just need practice. But please don't point the gun at anything aside from the floor or the target again."

"I won't, thank you."

Apparently, Aunt Alice didn't mind being scolded, as long as it was a lust-worthy male doing the scolding. Not a revelation I wanted to linger on.

Her relationship status was the one facet of her life she didn't have impeccably in place. She'd married young, kept her house in perfect order, borne her husband two perfect children, and served a home-cooked meal for him every evening at precisely six o'clock, until eleven years in, he'd left in the middle of the night never to be seen again.

The only explanation she ever got were the words "I can't do this anymore" scrawled on the magnetic notepad she kept on the fridge for grocery and to-do lists. Rumor had it that she'd been more upset that he tore off several pages of her scrupulous notes to find a blank page, than that he'd abandoned her with two young children and half a mortgage.

She'd secured a secretarial job the very next day and continued her stringent standards of perfection in every area of her life for the next twenty-five years up until the present day. But she'd never married again. Never even dated again, as far as I'd been led to believe. Now I wondered whether she was as adept at subterfuge as she was at everything else; there was obviously nothing wrong with her appetite for male company.

The woman in question had fired another ten shots, with three of them hitting her own target. I guess that counted as improvement. Maybe relationships were one of *two* things she didn't have down to a fine art.

I soon learned it didn't stop her giving advice on them. Connor was returning the weapons when she tackled me. "Etta tells me you were lucky enough to be dating Connor and you broke it off with him."

I sent Etta a nasty glare. "Why does everyone assume I was the one to break things off?"

"Because anyone can see he doesn't make decisions lightly," Aunt Alice informed me. "His type might take a long time to win over, but once they're on your side, they'll have your back for life. Not like your damn fool ex-husband, who said all the right things but let himself be swept away at the first sign of a storm. Connor might not fill your head with pretty words, but I'm telling you, he'll stand by you when the storm comes."

Actually, I thought it was more likely that he'd go outside and kick the storm's ass, or if it was too big for that, shove me down in the dirt and throw himself over me for protection.

"Take it from me, Isobel, that's not a trait to throw away."

It was like she'd flicked on a light. A very bright light that made my head hurt while illuminating the room. I knew down to the marrow of my bones that she was right. And now I understood why I'd said no to Levi.

He was charming, like my ex, and I couldn't trust him. Not that he'd ever shown even a hint of Steve's character weaknesses, but I'd been blind to them as well until he'd broken my heart, destroyed my new business, and set a loan shark on my tail to boot.

Maybe it was more accurate to say I couldn't trust myself. Levi could be the nicest guy in the world, and I'd never know, because I was too scared to give him a chance. While dispassionate, aloof Connor, who was about as hospitable as a glacier unless he warmed to you, had snuck past my defenses to become someone I might be able to trust with my heart. If he wanted it.

The problem was, our relationship had been a farce, and I'd never won him over to begin with.

11

THE FOUR OF US walked out to the dark parking lot. Etta stopped in front of her 1970s, buttercup-yellow Dodge Charger and scanned the other cars. "Where's your Corvette, Izzy?" she asked.

"I came with Connor."

"In that case, would you like a ride home?"

Being trapped in the Charger's tiny cabin with Aunt Alice was not desirous under any circumstances. Lucky I had reason to decline. "I'm afraid Connor and I still have work to do tonight. Would you mind telling Oliver to feed Meow?"

Etta wiggled her eyebrows at me. "Working real late, huh? Sure, I'll tell him."

"Thanks for suggesting this outing, Isobel," Aunt Alice said. "I don't know why you chose the shooting range when you didn't even pick up a weapon, but it was fun."

"You're very welcome." I tried to channel Dr. Kelly's serene smile and decided Oliver owed me big time. He'd sent me a total of five text messages containing the thumbs up emoji, so at least his evening had gone well.

"And don't forget what I told you," Aunt Alice added with a pointed glance toward Connor.

I wished I could forget. It would make tonight less awkward.

As I followed Connor to his SUV, I was glad I didn't have to drive. My skull throbbed, and the pain brought the threatening message back to the forefront of my mind. "What do we do if we can't find Earnest's backup flash drive?"

"Pretend to find and destroy it. Whoever's behind the threat is hardly a mastermind. Even if you found it and sent a video of its destruction, they couldn't be sure you hadn't copied it first. That's the problem with information. It's very hard to contain once it's been released. They must be hoping you're scared enough to do what they say."

"I guess I might be if I was a normal girl whose boyfriend had been murdered." Or if I wasn't so certain Connor would protect me.

"True." Connor eyed me. "Just as well you're anything but normal."

"Um. Thanks?"

He didn't respond.

I swallowed a couple of the painkillers Levi had given me and the antibiotics he'd supplied two days before. "Will Maria be at your house? Or is there any leftover food in the fridge? I haven't had dinner yet, and I'm starving."

"It must be difficult living in a state of perpetual hunger," Connor commented without answering my question.

"Only if I don't get fed."

He didn't take the hint.

"You know you didn't tell me whether there'd be food, right?"

He exhaled slowly through his nose. Not quite a sigh, but a show of exasperation all the same. "Maria left hours ago, but I'm sure we'll find you something."

My anxiety lessened. I don't do well on an empty stomach, and it had been a long day.

We pulled up to Connor's home in Beverly Hills. It was as I remembered it, an old Tudor-style mansion surrounded by a half acre of lawn and huge ancient trees. The maples and oaks had lost most of their leaves since I'd last been here, giving the whole place an austere appearance in the moonlight. Not that you could see much of the moon through the haze of smog that sat permanently above Los Angeles. It was something I could never quite get used to after growing up with the clean air and clear skies of Adelaide.

We entered through the solid timber front door, leaving the bronze lion-head knocker untouched. It opened into a wide, airy hallway, and I winced when we passed the vase I'd once vomited in after a poisoned meal, still decorating its own shelf. "You kept it?" I squeaked, pointing.

"I did tell you that vase belonged to my great-great-grandmother, right? If it makes you feel better, I had it professionally cleaned before putting it back."

For the next recruit he tested to vomit in. "Do you, uh, have a Shade-in-training at the moment?"

"No. And I wake up every day grateful for that."

I didn't know whether or not it was a dig at me, so I didn't reply. He flicked the lights on in the kitchen and went straight to the stainless steel fridge, leaving me to stare at his coffee machine. His real coffee machine. It was a well-used but undoubtedly well-maintained La Marzocco. How had he managed to deceive me so thoroughly?

Maybe *he* had spy training.

Okay, I was being dramatic, but it made me realize again how little I knew about him. So why did I trust him?

Probably because he always protects you.

Ugh. I couldn't believe Aunt Alice was right.

It was a shame it was too late for an espresso, but at least I'd been promised one tomorrow morning. And all the mornings after that, as long as I stayed on the case. "Do you have any decaf beans?" I asked. Decaf was never quite as good, but if the beans had been decaffeinated by the Swiss Water Process, it was a good way to drink coffee at night.

"No, sorry."

It figured. Connor was too tough to need decaf. Decaf is for humans who need to sleep. Not cyborgs.

"But I do have leftover green curry chicken."

"Sounds great."

He put it in the microwave, and a few minutes later we sat down at the dining table with steaming, fragrant bowls. The table was covered with a natural linen cloth and featured a centerpiece of three glass vases that had been filled with copper- and ivory-colored Christmas baubles.

"Maria's doing?" I asked.

Connor grunted and picked up his fork.

Sitting here brought back more memories. "You didn't poison the curry did you?"

It had been part of the process of assessing new Shades, and I wouldn't put it past him to treat me to a surprise for old times' sake. Especially if he'd found out I hadn't had a poisoned meal in three months.

His face didn't offer any clues. "I might need to check whether the head injury affected your abilities."

I swapped our bowls. Connor watched on, unconcerned. Not poisoned then? Or had he anticipated the switch? With an inward groan, I sniffed and tasted the first mouthful before swallowing. My stomach grumbled at the delay, but it would grumble even more if he'd poisoned it. I tasted another mouthful from a different section of the meal.

He hadn't poisoned it.

"You're such a jerk."

His expression turned smug. "This shouldn't be news to you by now."

I wolfed the bowl down. "Is there any more?" He began to get up, but I stopped him. "Don't worry. I can stick it in the microwave myself."

That way I wouldn't have to test for more poison.

When I returned to the table, Connor had finished his first bowl but made no move to fetch seconds.

"So," I said, tucking into my own seconds, "tell me something about yourself."

Perhaps if I learned more about the man, he'd lose some of his enigmatic appeal. With luck, it would help me think of him as an ordinary, tarnished human rather than a shiny, majestic cyborg.

Okay, I couldn't see myself ever thinking of him as ordinary. But at the very least, it might put us on more even footing.

"I'm a private investigator for the Taste Society," he said.

I paused in my shoveling. "Ha ha. Something I don't know."

He leaned toward me, his biting citrus and sun-warmed leather scent mingling pleasantly with the curry. "You really want to know something?"

I nodded, forgetting to breathe.

"Levi is wrong. I have an excellent bedside manner."

I spluttered. Connor smirked.

I didn't ask him any more questions after that. He seemed content to watch me while I finished eating. I wished he wouldn't. My abdomen was hot and tingly, and I was trying to convince myself it was from the spices.

Time to cut myself off for the evening. "Where am I sleeping? And can I have a shower?"

I'd showered this morning, but after spending hours in a funeral home, getting clubbed over the head, and watching Aunt Alice and Etta ogle Connor, I felt like I needed another one.

"I'll set up a bed for you in my room."

"What?" I assumed by the fact he was setting up a bed for me that it wasn't an invitation. Which was good because I didn't want it to be. "Don't you have about half a dozen guest rooms in this place?"

"Something like that. But I'm meant to be monitoring

you, and I'd prefer not to have to get up every few hours to do it."

"But—"

"If you object to sleeping on the floor, there's room in my bed."

I gave up. So much for cutting myself off. "The floor is fine."

"Good. I'll grab you a towel."

"You're so domestic."

He rose to his feet without deigning to respond, and I followed him out of habit. While the exterior of his home was traditional Tudor, the inside was a pleasing mix of modern white walls and bright, uncluttered spaces, paired with the original exposed dark timbers and floorboards. Paintings were his decoration of choice, with the occasional sculpture on a floating shelf. Anything less beautiful was minimized or tucked away. He took a towel from a concealed closet that I'd assumed was a normal part of the wall until two seconds ago. "You remember where the bathroom is."

He meant his personal bathroom as that was the one I'd used when pretending to be his girlfriend. But hell, if I had to sleep in his room, I guess I might as well use his en-suite. It was modern and spacious and had a fancy shower where the water poured from the ceiling. I was half-naked before I realized I didn't have any clean clothes to change into.

It was a situation I'd found myself in distressingly often when I had been Connor's Shade. Which reminded me that I'd finally prepared for it by stashing a spare pair of underwear in my bag. Because I hadn't cleaned out my bag since, they should still be there.

I rummaged, located them, shook off a bit of lint and one of Meow's feather toys, and held them up triumphantly. Point one to the disorganized, non-minimalists of the world.

Organized minimalists had no doubt scored plenty more than one point on me. Fortunately, they'd never clutter up their minds or homes with the means to keep track.

My scalp stung under the water, and I realized towel-drying my hair would be painful with all the bruising and swelling. I washed it gingerly and left it a touch shy of dripping. It'd do. Feeling clean and refreshed despite my head, I finger-brushed my teeth and called it good enough. I pulled on my "fresh" pair of undies. My full-length skirt and long-sleeved knit top weren't going to cut it as sleepwear, though, so I wrapped my towel around me and exited the bathroom.

Connor was expertly folding the sheets into hospital corners on the mattress that was now in the middle of his bedroom floor.

Wow. He really is domestic. "Can I borrow a T-shirt?"

His eyes fastened on the towel. I pressed my elbow harder into the side I'd tucked the end in, just in case it tried to jump free under the influence of his smoldering gaze.

Maybe he did still find me attractive.

The whole moment lasted less than a second before he noticed the claw marks.

"What happened to your arms?"

"Meow doesn't like Dudley."

"Are you taking antibiotics? Cat scratches can be nasty."

Sheesh, why did everyone know this but me?

"Yessir. Now can I have that T-shirt?"

"Sure." His eyes skimmed over me one more time before he went to fetch it from the wardrobe. I swear the damn thing was ironed. I returned to the bathroom and re-emerged a minute later, tugging the T-shirt down to cover the undies I was so proud of having. He was already in bed, presumably having brushed his teeth in another of his bathrooms. He was too well groomed to skip it.

Riled up as I was from our encounter, I was disappointed to miss learning what he wore to sleep. I could imagine anything from stately pajamas to full nudity. Maybe I shouldn't imagine the nudity.

His eyes tracked me as I walked to the mattress on the floor and slipped under the neatly made covers. "Thanks for saving me from sleeping at the medical facility," I said, trying to find a comfortable position for my sore head and my wanton body.

He flicked off the light switch. "I just hope you don't snore."

12

EVERYONE SHOULD wake up to the smell of freshly extracted espresso. Connor was already gone. He'd roused me twice overnight to check if I was alive and shine a flashlight in my eyes. Fortunately or unfortunately, I hadn't been able to see much of him in whatever he wore to bed with the aforementioned flashlight in my eyes. I also wasn't sure if he'd snored, given I'd slept like a hibernating bear despite all the reasons not to.

I really hoped I hadn't snored.

Dressed in the same outfit as yesterday, only with less makeup due to being limited to the mascara and lip gloss in my bag, I emerged from the bedroom.

Maria was the one responsible for the heavenly coffee scent. She hadn't gotten any taller since I'd seen her last, but neither had she lost any of her cheerful authority. I wondered, not for the first time, how many of Connor's secrets she knew. If I had to bet, I'd say a lot more than me.

"Espresso?" she asked me with a knowing smile. She had a handsome, oval face, dominated by a strong nose and shrewd eyes the color of the darkest French roasted coffee beans. When she smiled, you forgot about the nose.

"Please," I said, wondering whether Connor had passed on my "tell Maria I love her" message.

She went to the machine, her bright floral blouse offering a counterpoint to the practical black apron and the slicked-back inky hair.

"How's Armando?" I asked her.

She and her husband had been married for thirty-eight years, and her entire being lit up like a Disney Princess meeting her prince whenever she talked about him. "He is good. We love cold weather." She beamed as she expertly ground and tamped the coffee, then attached the portafilter to the machine. "What does wolf say? All better for snuggling." She gave me a wink.

Laughing, I carried my cream-laden short black to the dining room where Connor was already seated. "Do you think you'll ever find what Maria and Armando have?" I asked him.

He was reading something on his digital tablet and didn't bother to look up. "What do you think they have?"

I shrugged, embarrassed. "Someone to snuggle with every winter, I guess."

"Depends whether it has to be the same someone."

I felt a twinge of jealousy. I was far from grateful to Aunt Alice for bringing those feelings to the forefront of my mind.

"What about you?" he asked, attention still on the tablet.

I sipped my espresso before answering and felt instantly better. "By your definition, I've already found it."

He looked up.

"Meow and Dudley make excellent snuggle buddies."

Amusement shone in his eyes. "Does Levi know who you turned him down for?"

"Well he did treat my cat scratches, so he might have some idea." I pushed away the nagging voice that said I'd made a mistake in saying no and took another blissful sip. "What's the plan this morning?"

Connor slid over the tablet he'd been so reluctant to look up from. The headline leaped out at me.

BusiLeaks Whistle-Blower Murdered!

"The LAPD informed the media late last night," Connor said, "which means you'll likely be contacted by reporters looking to pad out their stories today. Keep your responses to a minimum. You can express sorrow, but don't talk about the case, period."

My pleasant morning bubble popped. "Got it."

"Beyond that, we'll talk to Mr. Massey and find out if he knows anything about that flash drive. If we're lucky, he'll know more than you did."

Jerk.

Thirty minutes later I jogged up the stairs to my apartment for a change of clothes. Okay, I jogged up half the stairs before I got a stitch. I told myself it was the exercising-on-a-full-stomach thing rather than the totally unfit thing and hoped Connor wasn't watching from the car. Surely he had better things to do.

Oliver was asleep, so there was no need to explain why I hadn't come home last night. I put the rescued muffins in the kitchen, petted Meow for a minute, and threw on a new outfit. Then I made a quick detour to the bathroom to brush my teeth with a real toothbrush and add some product to tame my wild hair. I thought about applying some extra makeup, but since my revised position on the case involved hiding in the car while Connor interviewed people, decided against it.

My phone buzzed a second before someone knocked on the door. Figuring Connor must have come up to see what was taking so long, I opened the door while digging through my bag for the phone.

A camera flashed, a video camera blinked at me, and three microphones were thrust at my face. "Isobel Avery?"

I blinked back at the cameras.

"How do you feel about Earnest Dunst's death?"

"How long were you dating Earnest?"

"Is it true you found his body?"

"Did Mr. Dunst leave a will?"

"I . . ."

Everyone fell silent to hear what I had to say. The problem was, I didn't know what to say.

"Um." *Great start.* "Earnest Dunst was a good man. A very good man. His death is a tragedy. And I don't feel up to talking about it right now. I'm sorry."

I tried to shut the door but the microphones got in my way.

"Who do you think might have killed Earnest?"

"Will anyone continue his work?"

"How did you meet him when he almost never left his house?"

"Are the police treating you as a suspect?"

"I'm sorry. No further comments." This time, I managed to pull the door shut.

Wow. How did anyone deal with being famous?

I remembered I'd been rummaging through my bag for my phone and recommenced the search. The text I'd heard come in was from Connor.

Press are about to knock on your door.

Perfect.

I sent him a reply.

Didn't see your message until it was too late. Do you think they'll go away?

Oliver came out of his bedroom. "What's going on? Why are there reporters on our doorstep?"

My phone rang before I could answer him. Etta. "Did you know there are reporters outside?"

I blew out a breath. "You should come over when they leave. I might as well tell you and Oliver at the same time."

The next ten minutes seemed to take at least twenty. Oliver had a shower. I fed Meow, put on extra makeup despite it being too late now, and made three cups of tea. I also texted Connor again.

I have to do damage control with Etta and Oliver. Could be a while. Wanna come up?

He replied right away.

I'll sit this one out.

Jerk.

Eventually the news crews realized I wasn't coming back out until they left, or they got a more exciting proposition than Earnest's unknown, uncooperative, and ineloquent girlfriend. Etta was over thirty seconds later, blue eyes sparkling with excitement. She was decked out in yellow slacks, a black fitted jacket, and a stylish patterned scarf. I couldn't help but think she would have made a far better picture for the cameras.

I handed her a cup of tea, and we sat down at the table with Oliver who was in his usual T-shirt and worn-out jeans. He'd recently started collecting novelty T-shirts and now showed them off at least a couple of times a week. Today's said "Save the Chubby Unicorns" with an image of a rhino underneath. It was very tame by his standards. I assumed that was for Henrietta and Aunt Alice's sake.

"Do you know what this is about?" Etta asked him.

"No clue."

"How is that possible? She's *your* housemate."

"You're the one who usually knows everything about everyone in this building," he said. "You must be losing your touch."

They jostled each other the same way eight-year-old siblings would and turned to me expectantly.

Oh boy. "You're not going to like this," I told them. "I've been dating someone."

"What?"

"Who?"

"When?"

"Someone you might have heard of. The man behind BusiLeaks. You know, that whistle-blowing website about American businesses?"

"The one that died a few days ago?" Etta asked.

"Uh. Yes. And now the police are treating his death as

suspicious. Which is why the press were here this morning." I chewed my lip, unsure how to continue.

"Well, hell." Etta said, all the air gone out of her. "I really thought you and Connor were getting back together."

"Why didn't you tell us?" Oliver asked. "We know your job is confidential, but surely your boyfriend isn't!" He crossed his arms and managed to look indignant and dejected at the same time, even with a cartoon rhinoceros on his shirt.

He had a point. I could've told them about the "dating" Earnest part, given that it was congruent with my cover. But with Earnest keeping such a low profile, and Etta crestfallen over my breakup with Connor, I figured it was easier not to. There was no reason for them to ever find out. Or so I'd thought.

"Sorry guys. I know I should've told you. I just . . . Well it was new, and I couldn't believe it myself and you both liked Connor so much . . ."

Their gazes were not understanding.

"Um. Wanna try my white-chocolate-and-raspberry muffins?"

"Yes," they said in unison.

"But you can't buy us off with food," Etta added. "We're very upset with you."

"Of course," I agreed. "But they're pretty good." I fled to fetch them.

Three muffins later, there were fewer glares being cast my way. I figured it was as much as I could expect for a while. I brought over another pair of sugary peace offerings. "I'd appreciate it if you didn't mention this to Aunt Alice."

"If those news crews were anything to go by, your face is about to be splashed all over the papers," Etta said.

Damn. She was right. Probably beside a shot of Oliver's *Chrismyass* poster knowing my luck. "True. But I mean, if you could pretend you knew I was dating him—"

"Forget it."

"I'm not lying to Henrietta!"

"Okay." It was fair enough, and I couldn't find it within me to argue. "Well, I'm sorry again for keeping all this from you. But I need to run."

Etta's eyes shot up from the muffin. "Wait. I was hoping you could take Dudley today. I'm having some rooms repainted, and I don't want him to be stuck inside with the fumes. I'd take him out myself, but I have to make sure the painters know what they're doing."

"Well, I'm working with Connor again today." I went to the window and peered down to the street below. He hadn't moved from his SUV, but I saw my Corvette had been miraculously returned. I didn't know if I'd be able to miraculously squeeze eighty pounds of Dudley inside though, even if Connor would let me drive it. "I'll see what he thinks about having a dog in his car."

I jogged across the road to where he was parked and tapped on his window. Sure, I could have called him, but it was a relief to get out of the house.

He rolled the window down. "Glad to see Etta and Oliver decided to let you live."

"No thanks to you. Etta might have gone easy on me if she'd had your hot body in front of her to fantasize about."

"You think I have a hot body?"

I rolled my eyes. "Etta does."

He looked a little less smug about that.

"Can I drive my car today?" I asked.

"No. It's too conspicuous, and we're trying to make your movements invisible, remember? From Hunt as well as the press."

"I was afraid you'd say that. In that case, how would you feel about having Dudley in your SUV?" I eyed the spotless interior and silently amended my question to *your immaculate SUV.* Better not to draw his attention to it.

"Sure."

"Really?"

He gave an infinitesimal shrug. "Greyhounds don't have the normal dog odor because of the lack of oil in their skin. They don't shed much either."

I stared at Mr. Encyclopedia as if he'd sprouted a second head.

"Some friends of mine have greyhounds," he said.

"Wait, you have friends?"

He ignored me. As he should have. Yet I genuinely had trouble picturing Connor in a normal, leisure setting with a group of mates and their dogs.

"Right, I'll tell Etta the good news."

I didn't have to go far. She, Oliver, and Dudley were waiting at the bottom of the stairs. At least this way I wouldn't have to ask Connor to carry Dudley down them. I just hoped they weren't conspiring against me, plotting revenge.

"I packed a few of his things," Etta said, passing me a bulging tote bag. "And here's his bed to give him somewhere soft to lie down."

"Uh, thanks," I said, shouldering the bag and gathering the massive bed under my arm so I had a spare hand for Dudley's leash.

Oliver nudged Etta. "And also, we're sorry your boyfriend died."

"Yeah," Oliver chimed in, "we're still mad at you, but we want to be supportive too. So let us know if you need, well, anything."

13

THE SUV HAD PLENTY OF ROOM for Dudley, the soft bed, and a whole bag of bits and pieces Etta had given me. We rolled down Adams Boulevard with his head sticking out the window, nose twitching, ears flapping, and tongue lolling. I pretended not to notice the occasional bit of drool landing on Connor's pristine door panels.

A block away from Jay's place, Connor pulled over to the curb and handed me a transmitter with a headset attached. "This will allow you to listen in. It has a range of about two blocks, so if you take Dudley for a walk, you won't be able to go far. Stay out of direct sight of Mr. Massey's building in case any police or reporters are about."

I could hear the faint sound of Connor's footsteps and breathing as he walked to Jay's beach bungalow unit. Dudley had lain down on his bed and looked utterly content, but the sun was creeping out from behind the clouds, my stomach was creeping over the sides of my waistband, and walking with Dudley seemed like a whole lot more fun than exercising by myself. I dug through the bag Etta supplied and retrieved the leash, some dried liver treats, and poop bags.

The poop bags gave me a moment's pause, but I shook off the excuse, stuffed them into my pocket, and clipped on Dudley's leash.

Dudley sprung to his feet and leaped out of the car without hesitating. It was a two-and-a-half-foot drop, but apparently that was nothing compared to the evils of stairs. He stopped halfway up the curb to sniff a patch of concrete, and I had the sinking realization that he might see curbs as steps. From what Etta had told me, he could go up but not down. I was so caught up in thinking about how to get around this potential problem that I started at the sound of voices in my ear.

"Mr. Massey? I'm Connor Stiles, a consultant with the LAPD. I have a few questions for you."

"I already spoke to Commander Hunt about what I know yesterday," Jay protested.

"We have new information."

"Right. I guess you better come in then. You'll have to excuse the mess. I'm in the middle of moving."

Dudley didn't hesitate to follow me up or down the curb, which meant one isolated step was a surmountable obstacle. I gave him a palmful of treats in relief. Then we strolled along the sidewalk, with plenty of stops and starts for sniffs and letting all the other dogs know he'd been in the area.

"I'll get straight to the point, Mr. Massey," Connor said. "What do you know about Earnest's digital backup system?"

"He kept all his important data on a few hard drives as far as I'm aware. He didn't trust cloud storage—um, storing stuff online that is—he was always worried about security. He used one computer for gaming and Internet stuff, and a second one for his work, which he kept offline to make it impossible to hack."

"Do you know anything about a flash drive?"

Dudley didn't care about the flash drive. He thought the ginger cat on top of the fence post was way more interesting. Especially when this one wasn't hissing at him.

"Oh yeah, possibly," Jay said. "Years ago he used to carry a flash drive around with him as an extra level of backup. It didn't have everything on it, of course, so it was just the most important stuff. But that was before he became agoraphobic. I don't know if he kept the habit. It would've been a bit superfluous with him always being in the same place as his hard drives."

"Where did he used to keep it?"

"His wallet maybe? I think he tried having it in his pocket for a while, but it wound up in the washing machine, and flash drives weren't as cheap back then."

"Okay. Good."

Oh no. This wasn't good. Dudley was hunkering down to do number two, and the bravado I'd summoned up in the car had faded. Weren't poop bags meant to be biodegradable? How hygienic were they? Had it been tested?

"Why the interest in the flash drive?" Jay asked.

"We were hoping it would reveal what he was working on. I know Commander Hunt already asked, but are you sure you don't have any ideas about what he was looking into? Anything at all?"

"Actually, I've been thinking about it ever since you guys asked, and I don't know if it means anything, but I did glimpse the company name Aptech on his screen one time. It stuck in my mind because we both worked there about eight years ago when we were starting out. It's where we met."

"When did you see Aptech on his screen?"

"I'm not sure exactly. Around a month or so?"

"What did you and Earnest do when you worked for them?"

"Nothing important. Mostly coding for computer applications that don't exist anymore. It was a different company back then. They were a small player developing applications for third parties. Now they're the lead developer for what's supposed to be a revolutionary new operating system for the Pearl smartphones that're aiming to take on Apple in the US."

I wondered if this revolutionary operating system might be able to pick up dog poop. Praying the bags were hygienic, I bent down next to the steaming, aromatic pile. Dudley stared at me like I was nuts. "Yeah well, I'm not the one who pooped on the street," I told him.

Ignoring Dudley and all my instincts, I scooped up the gift and tied the bag shut. Even if the bags were hygienic, they weren't smell-proof. Dudley tugged me forward, and I started looking for a trash can.

"Did you remember anything else since speaking with Commander Hunt?"

"Well, Earnest's girlfriend might be worth checking out. The timing seems suspicious to me. She flounced into his life about two months ago, having absolutely nothing in common with him, and now he's dead."

I *flounced* along the sidewalk and resisted clenching my fists because I didn't want to break open the poop bag. Except maybe on Jay's stupid face.

"We'll be looking into every angle, Mr. Massey," Connor said.

Did I imagine the frost in his tone?

"Can you tell me what you were doing yesterday between twelve thirty and one p.m.?"

Oh. That was when I was smacked over the head.

"Yesterday? What happened yesterday?"

If Jay was feigning ignorance, he was convincing, at least over audio. But it didn't lessen my desire to smack *him* over the head.

"Please answer the question, Mr. Massey."

"Right. Um. I would've been picking up the keys to my new apartment. From the real estate manager. I can give you her details if you want?"

"Yes, thanks."

So my mystery head basher wasn't Jay, and he didn't have any actionable information for us on the flash drive. But perhaps we had a new lead that was worth investigating.

I tried to use that to soften my feelings toward Jay. No doubt I'd have to face him a bunch more times before this was over, and being mad at him for a comment I should never have overheard wasn't helpful. Besides, Earnest had loved him and the bond was mutual. Jay had once camped out overnight for some fancy, new, limited edition game console just to save Earnest waiting the three to five days it would've taken to have it posted. Remembering that took the edge off my anger.

Connor wrapped up the interview, while Dudley and

I prowled the streets, looking for a trash can. We passed a fatter than usual Santa, two elves, one of whom had a serious wedgie, and a big guy on a Harley with antlers attached to his helmet. No trash can.

The SUV came into view before I'd managed to dispose of the bag. Somehow I didn't think Connor would appreciate my having it in the car. Greyhounds might not have the normal doggy odor, but it doesn't extend to their poop.

In a moment of inspiration, I lifted up the back window wiper and stuck the bag under it. Then Dudley and I hopped inside, feeling pleased with ourselves.

IN KEEPING with my recent luck, it began to rain on our way to meet with the CEO of Aptech. I mean soaked-to-the-skin-in-thirty-seconds rain. It had drizzled twice in November and a handful of times in the past few weeks, but this was the first significant rainfall in months.

"I need my wipers," Connor said. "Next trash can we see, you'll have to get out and move that bag."

Of course.

The pouring rain and the gloom it dragged in with it made it hard to spot trash cans. Traffic ground to a standstill. Dudley was happy to have the windows rolled up. Connor phoned Hunt and updated him loudly over the drumming water on the roof. Unsurprisingly, Hunt opted to stay in his office rather than meet Connor at Aptech.

At last I spotted a trash can fifty meters ahead. We oozed our way toward it with the speed of a slug, and I hoped in vain the rain might stop before we reached it. It didn't. I stepped out into an inch of water over the road, instantly drenching my suede boots and the socks inside them, and disposed of the bag as fast as I could. Back inside, I watched the water run off my hair and clothes to form a puddle on Connor's seat.

He didn't say anything. Just turned up the heat at the same time as turning on the rear wiper.

My phone rang, and I fished it out of my pocket, grateful it hadn't drowned. "Hello?"

"Isobel Avery? I'm Carrie Williams from One Two Three News, and we want to write a story about the real man behind BusiLeaks. This is a chance for you to—"

"I'm not interested, thanks." I disconnected the call.

Forty minutes later, with the heater blasting, I had evolved to merely damp, Connor had stripped off his jacket and still looked too hot, and we'd arrived at Aptech's headquarters. If it weren't for the rain, the drive to Playa Vista, Silicon Beach, would've taken half the time.

On the way, I'd had three more phone calls from different reporters. My guess was they'd all fled to their desks and were making calls until the weather cleared. From here on in, I was letting any unknown numbers go to voice mail.

The rain stopped seconds before Connor got out of the car. Of course.

Aptech headquarters was a discreet two-story building made of prefabricated concrete panels and mirrored windows. I watched as Connor was swallowed by the shiny sliding doors. The CEO would be on the top floor, and he apparently needed an elevator because I could hear the quiet dings of the buttons and the muted hum as it rose. Then an attractive, feminine voice said, "Mr. Stiles, Mr. Coleman will just be a moment. Can I get you a drink while you wait?"

"No, thank you."

There was a minute of the soft clacking of fingers on a keyboard. I googled the CEO's photo while I waited. Strawberry blond hair swept across his head from a side part, crowning a face with tanned skin that looked almost baby smooth. An odd effect on a middle-aged man. He was smiling, close-lipped at the camera, but his eyebrows had a natural arch to them that transformed the gesture into one of self-satisfied amusement at your expense.

The clacking on the keyboard stopped. "Mr. Coleman is ready for you now. Please follow me."

"Thank you, Ms. McCarthy," said a new voice, this one slick and masculine. It fit the man in the photo perfectly.

"Mr. Stiles. My assistant tells me you're a consultant for the LAPD? What can I do to help the boys in blue?"

"You can tell me what you're working on," Connor said in his warm and personable style. I shared an exasperated look with Dudley. Maybe I should buy him the book *How to Win Friends and Influence People* for Christmas.

Coleman chuckled, but it sounded a tad forced. "What aren't we working on? You might want to be more specific, or we'll be here all day."

"What are you working on that would concern Earnest Dunst, the founder of BusiLeaks."

"Never heard of him, so I couldn't begin to postulate."

"That's a shame, given I know for a fact you have a leak at Aptech who contacted Mr. Dunst about your misconduct."

This time the chuckle sounded more genuine. I wondered why since I expected the opposite. "Nice bluff, Mr. Stiles, but it sounds to me like you've got nothing."

Connor's voice turned lower and quieter. "I'll tell you what I've got, Mr. Coleman. I've got a murder victim who was known to be investigating your company. Which gives you a big fat motive."

"Wait. Mr. Dunst is dead?" He sounded surprised yet thoughtful. Like he was moving chess pieces in his mind, working out how the removal of this pawn affected the game.

"A minute ago you told me you'd never heard of him."

"Right—"

"We can play this two ways. I can mention Aptech to the press, who are slavering for a good story, and they'll splash your company name over the front pages until there's so much speculation over why Earnest Dunst was investigating you that it won't matter whether you're guilty or not. Or you can cooperate."

"Here's a third option," Coleman said. "I could sue you for defamation."

"You could try, but I wouldn't need to tell the press anything I couldn't prove. Namely, that Mr. Dunst was working on something to do with Aptech when he was murdered. The press and BusiLeaks's reputation will do the rest."

"What proof do you have?"

"Mr. Dunst's computer."

Coleman snorted. "Now I know you're bluffing, and I've got better things to do than waste my time with your strong-arm bullshit tactics. Let yourself out, or I'll have my security assist you."

Chair legs scraped on what I imagined was polished concrete flooring. "This isn't over."

The doors must have been soft-close because I didn't hear it shut. I couldn't believe Connor had gone through it gently.

"Thanks for visiting Aptech, Mr. Stiles," said the same attractive, feminine voice as before. "Have a wonderful Christmas."

Connor grunted at her.

My amusement at their interaction kept me from fidgeting too much as I waited for him to return to the car. As soon as he sat down, I blurted, "Coleman knows about the hard drives being wiped." It was the only way he could've been confident that we had no proof on Earnest's computer.

"Yes."

"Which means he organized it. Unless the Taste Society has a leak too."

Connor clicked on his seat belt. "I'm going to bet on the former."

"Then do you think he organized a hit on Earnest as well?" I hadn't quite come to terms with the reality of that. Could this baby-skinned CEO really be behind Earnest's death?

"Chances are good. But the time between the murder and the wiping of the files bothers me." He looked me over. "If your memory of the screensaver is correct, the data was erased between eight thirty and eleven a.m., hours after Earnest's death."

"I'm positive Earnest's screensaver was on when I was looking for him that morning, but I've been wondering about the timeline too. Could the murderer have been busy getting rid of evidence for six hours?"

"Unlikely."

"Well. If Coleman is behind it, he'd hire a professional hitman right? What if the hired guy didn't have the skills to wipe the computer properly? Coleman would've wanted to make sure it was done properly, so he could have organized a second person to deal with the hard drives when the coast was clear."

"It's as good a theory as any I've come up with. He might've even had someone from Aptech do the erasure part since there's no shortage of tech experts in the company. The problem is we don't have a scrap of evidence to hang it on. And we need evidence to confront Coleman again. We need that flash drive."

"Have you gone through Earnest's personal affects? Flash drives come in all sorts of shapes and sizes. Is it possible that whoever processed it didn't recognize it as something that stores data? Or didn't realize its significance?"

"It's worth trying. And thanks to your hard head, the intruder didn't get to finish searching Earnest's apartment. Perhaps we should. Even if Earnest usually kept it on him, he could've taken it off for some reason."

I wasn't sure how I felt about the hard head comment. "But how can I help with either when Commander Hunt is waiting for his chance to toss me in jail?"

AS I COULDN'T PARTICIPATE in the search, Connor dropped me home. Unfortunately, being home meant I'd have to somehow convince Dudley and Meow to see nose to nose. Or at least stop Meow from lacerating Dudley's nose.

He climbed up the stairs all by himself, which was just as well seeing as I was already juggling his bed and goody bag. My clothes were almost dry, but my suede boots squelched with each step. At the top, I gave Dudley a pat and a few of the treats Etta had supplied. Maybe the triumph would help him be brave in the face of Meow.

My lofty ideals of bravery fled when I spotted Aunt Alice, Henrietta, and Oliver through the window. Their gazes were glued on the television, so they hadn't seen me.

Much like I had with Mr. Black, I flattened myself against the wall and considered my options.

I could do the grown-up thing by going inside and making a nice lunch for everyone.

I could buy breathing apparatuses for Dudley and me and go hang out at Etta's place until they left.

Or I could try to squeeze Dudley in my Corvette and disappear into the horizon. Never mind that snails were outpacing the traffic since the earlier downpour.

The last option was seriously tempting until I

remembered I'd have to carry Dudley down the stairs first. But he might've gained confidence from our curb-hopping adventure. I walked him across the landing and started down the steps, pretending it was no big deal as I knew dogs took cues from body language.

Dudley wasn't fooled.

"C'mon, Dudley. Stairs are nothing compared to the horrors of that apartment." I leaned down to appeal to him. "You remember Meow don't you? That fiery spitball that had you trembling behind Etta's legs?"

Dudley licked me on the chin and stared at me with his gentle brown eyes, trusting me to look after him. Whether that meant protecting him from the demon cat or carrying him down the unconquerable stairs was immaterial.

Crap.

"Should we hang out here on Etta's outdoor sofa?"

It began to drizzle.

"Ugh. Fine. Why are grown-up decisions always the least appealing options?" I towed Dudley back across the landing, pasted a smile on my face, and opened the front door. "Hi, everyone. I was about to make some lunch. Would you like some?"

Oliver's face brightened, Henrietta's darkened, and Aunt Alice's turned to Dudley with the kind of look she normally reserved for me. I'd forgotten how much she disliked animals.

"Lunch would be great," Oliver said. "We're watching a documentary about LA, but I've seen it before, so I'll give you a hand."

I was shocked he would voluntarily leave her worshipfulness, the oh-so-poised Henrietta, to help me cook. Then again, his ability to make the most of his couch time with her was severely hampered by Aunt Alice chaperoning them. She was the ultimate wet blanket.

Given Meow tended to be Oliver's second shadow whenever he was home, I crouched in front of Dudley and petted him in preparation for their arrival. Except she didn't appear. "Where's Meow? Is she okay?"

"Yeah. She's hanging out in my bedroom." Oliver squatted beside me to greet Dudley and lowered his voice. "Mrs. Sloan doesn't like her much, and it seems the feeling is mutual."

"I thought cats are usually attracted to people that don't like them."

"Well, Meow is smarter than most cats."

"Because she can say her own name, you mean?"

"Exactly."

I looked over to Aunt Alice sitting primly on the couch. "Are you sure you want her as your mother-in-law?"

"Why not? As long as she lives overseas."

I grinned and cuffed his shoulder. "So disrespectful."

"And wise," he added.

Well, except for the choice of girlfriend. "Sure. Whatever you say."

I changed out of my soggy boots and set up Dudley's bed next to me in the kitchen. It meant we had to keep stepping around him, but at least he was safe from both Meow and Aunt Alice. He settled onto it following a few cursory sniffs, and I wondered if he could possibly be tired after all his sleeping in the car. He did seem to like lying down more than any other dog I'd ever met. Or maybe he'd scented Meow and concluded it was safer not to explore.

We decided on mushroom and bacon risotto for lunch. Normally I'd throw all the ingredients in the rice cooker and walk away, but today I put it in a saucepan on the stove where I would have to stir it constantly. Anything for an excuse not to join Aunt Alice and Henrietta on the couch.

The documentary and risotto finished around the same time, and we gathered at the table. "How are you enjoying LA?" I asked as I dished out the food.

My question was aimed at keeping this conversation on topics other than my failings.

"It's very nice," said Aunt Alice.

Henrietta and Oliver shared a secret smile while she was distracted.

"But I was sorry to hear about your boyfriend's death." I felt the weight of her gaze. "You know, the one you didn't tell us about."

The spoon I was dishing with froze in midair. "I didn't want to ruin your visit. With such heavy news, I mean."

"Nonsense, Isobel. We're here to support you, aren't we, Henrietta?"

"Of course," Henrietta parroted, but she made sure to meet my eyes and shake her head ever so slightly. Which I took to mean: *drop dead.*

"And you need all the support you can get when it comes to men," Aunt Alice continued, oblivious to her perfect daughter's rebellion. "First you pick a man who could charm the pants off anyone and probably did, then you win over the strong, steady type and leave him for no apparent reason, and finally you wind up with a seemingly safe option, a smart agoraphobic who'd never have a chance to cheat on you or run off, only he gets murdered. When is his funeral being held?"

I studied her face but could see no sign of mockery. There was plenty in Henrietta's though. "The funeral's Wednesday. But it's not necessary for you to come. You're supposed be enjoying your hard-earned holiday. And you never had the chance to meet him."

She treated me to one of her disapproving sighs. "Now whose fault is that?"

As Earnest passed away before she touched down in LA, I thought that was harsh.

"We'll be there." Her tone said the issue was closed.

“Okay. Um. Thanks.” Aunt Alice was the last person I’d want at the funeral. She’d no doubt find fault with my outfit, my not-waterproof-enough mascara, and the entire service if she learned from Mrs. Dunst that I’d helped plan it. And if it weren’t for Henrietta’s complete disinterest in me, she’d be just as bad. But how could I argue?

It was an event I was already dreading. On top of the heartache, I felt like a fraud pretending to be Earnest’s grieving girlfriend to so many people. It was weird that I’d have to play the role more convincingly at his funeral than any day I’d spent with him.

“Etta and I discussed it earlier, and we’re coming too,” Oliver said.

Fantastic. I contemplated smothering myself in the pot of risotto. Now everyone would witness my deceit.

14

I WAS UP TO MY ELBOWS in suds washing dishes when Etta called me. I'd had six more calls from reporters that I'd ignored and had been wondering how Connor was coming along in his search for Earnest's flash drive. I used my nose to answer the phone and put it on loudspeaker.

"Whereabouts are you and Dudley?" Etta asked. "I've had the windows open and the fan going all day, so I think he might be able to come home now."

I eyed the stack of dishes and the happy trio at the dining table conversing about Aunt Alice's extraordinary marksmanship. "We'll be right over."

Etta opened the door to my knock and lunged straight for Dudley. "Hello, my favorite boy! I've missed you, oh yes I have. Have you been a good boy?"

Dudley was equally exuberant. His whole body wiggled with glee, from his pointy nose all the way down to the tip of his tail, which whipped me like an expertly wielded tea towel.

I rubbed my leg and smiled, waiting for one of them to remember I was there.

Etta finally looked up. "Oh, Izzy, nice to see you too. Come in and have a hot drink with me." She was bundled up for the weather in a red fur-lined coat and knee-high tan leather boots. The cold and Dudley's kisses brought a becoming glow to her cheeks.

"How'd it go today?" I asked, following her inside. Despite the open windows, the paint fumes were potent, like when I'd visited Jay a couple of days ago.

"Oh good. They only got the first coat done of course, but I'm happy with their work. I trust they'll finish it off just as neatly, so I think Dudley and I will go on a half-day trip tomorrow."

I was kind of disappointed I wouldn't need to babysit Dudley again, but I didn't admit it. Best she thought I'd done her a favor. After the secret boyfriend fiasco, I needed all the brownie points I could get.

"Can I see what you're having done?" I asked.

"Sure. It's the bedrooms and bathroom. I had them painted when I first moved in but always wished I'd chosen a lighter shade."

"So if Dudley was your Christmas present to yourself, what does the repainting come under?" I teased.

"My other Christmas present to myself."

I couldn't argue with that.

Curiosity plucked at me as we made our way toward her bedroom. It saw so much more action than mine, and I couldn't even begin to guess at her decorating choices.

Everything had been shifted away from the walls, but the design was easy to make out. A timber floating bed with a low headboard took pride of place, with a simple white duvet and two charcoal pillows. None of those fussy throw cushions. Plain matching timber bedside tables held a few books, and reading lights were suspended by black cords from the ceiling. A huge peace lily plant grew in a white marble pot to the left of the bed. The effect was elegant, modern, and gender-neutral, with the barest touch of femininity lent by a faux fur throw at the foot of the mattress.

She should have been an interior designer.

There was no sign of complex sexual equipment, but if she owned any, it could have been hidden behind the built-in wardrobe. While Etta wasn't the type to hide such things, she may have done it out of courtesy to avoid intimidating the workmen.

"The paint is dry to the touch now, so I took the throw sheets off," Etta said, "but it does smell stronger in here doesn't it? Maybe Dudley and I should sleep in the living room tonight."

I finally turned my attention to the walls. The pale gray paint, with streaks of the darker shade showing through, niggled something in the back of my mind.

All of a sudden I knew who'd erased Earnest's hard drives.

I just didn't know why.

I drained my cup of tea as quickly as possible, agreed they should sleep in the living room, and excused myself. Then I called Connor. "I think it was Jay Massey."

"What was Jay Massey?"

"Who erased Earnest's hard drives."

"Start from the beginning."

"Well, after our conversation about the possibility of the computers being wiped by a second person, I still thought the timing was weird. If Coleman had organized both the hitman and the computer guy, why send the computer guy during waking hours when someone could walk in on him? So then I thought, what if he only organized the computer guy? Maybe the computer guy was monitoring the house, waiting for an opportunity, and the murderer happened to give him one. But who, aside from the killer, knew the apartment was empty? The only people I could come up with was me, Mrs. Dunst, and Jay since I called them when I was trying to figure out where Earnest was."

"I'm with you so far."

"I knew Mrs. Dunst didn't do it because she was looking for Earnest at the same time I was, but Jay was busy. Mrs. Dunst told me yesterday that he was in the middle of painting something for the landlord, which is why he didn't help us search. But when I went over to Etta's, I remembered that Jay was applying the *first* coat of paint the day I talked to him. It's possible he had to paint something else for the landlord, but it's not a normal end-of-lease requirement, so it isn't likely. Which means it *is* likely he lied about what he was doing the morning of Earnest's disappearance."

"Okay, but—"

"It makes sense. Why else would he lie? He told us himself that he used to work for Aptech. If he and Coleman knew each other, Coleman could have convinced him to wipe Earnest's computers somehow. He had a key, the technical knowledge to do it, and could've simply waited for one of the rare occasions Earnest left the house. He was the perfect choice."

Connor was silent for a moment. "So the murder was unrelated to the data loss?"

"That's the part I can't figure out. No way was Jay involved in Earnest's death. You should've seen them together. Plus he was a mess after he heard Earnest was gone and furious when Mrs. Dunst told him Earnest was murdered. But that morning before Earnest was found, both Mrs. Dunst and Jay thought he'd fallen off the wagon again. So Jay might've seen it as a good opportunity to access his hard drives, having no idea he'd been killed."

"It's plausible. Would Mr. Massey be susceptible to bribes?"

"I don't know. He loved Earnest, I'm sure of it, but Earnest lived in that budget apartment because it was easier for him to stay where it was familiar and he didn't care about material things anyway. Whereas Jay wanted a nicer place. Which is why he's moving, and keeping up with the latest technology isn't cheap. Plus he's come into some money lately. He claimed it was because his YouTube marketing course has been selling well, but he could've lied."

"Right. Then let's go see if we can convince Mr. Massey that we know more than we do."

DUSK HAD FALLEN over LA by the time we arrived back in University Park. We stopped a block away again, on a different street, and I stayed inside with my transmitter and headphones while Connor headed to Jay's. His search for the flash drive had come up empty, so this was our sole lead. And it was admittedly a stretch. Lucky Connor was good at the bluffing thing.

"You again?" Jay sounded peeved. "I hope you're here because you've found the bastard behind this."

"I suggest you invite me in to have this conversation inside."

I listened to the creak of floorboards as they walked down the passageway again and then the sound of chairs being pulled out for sitting on.

"We know it was you," Connor said.

"What? What are you talking about?" Jay still sounded peeved, but his voice was an octave higher than before.

"You erased Earnest's files. You lied to Mrs. Dunst about having to paint and then let yourself in with your spare key and deleted everything while you knew his apartment was empty."

"That's—"

"Before you finish that sentence, think about this. Even if you had nothing to do with the murder, lying right now is an obstruction of justice in a homicide investigation." Connor paused for a beat. "You don't look like you'd fare well in prison. Of course, if you were involved with the murder, then you should probably keep silent about the hard drives."

Thirty seconds ticked by.

"How did you know? Did Earnest have cameras installed or something?"

"What did Coleman offer you?"

I held my breath, hoping Connor's stab in the dark wouldn't puncture the hot air balloon we were flying this interrogation on.

"A hundred grand in cash. But it wasn't why I did it, I swear. I wouldn't betray Earnest even for a hundred grand."

A hundred grand cash would pay off my debt to the loan shark in full. I could go home to Australia, away from all this subterfuge, machinations, and death, and be with my loved ones. Though I'd dearly miss Etta, Oliver, Meow, and Dudley. Okay, and maybe Connor.

"Then why did you betray him?"

"To save him! That's what I thought I was doing anyway, but maybe I was too late, or maybe whoever was behind this never intended to leave him alive."

"Explain," Connor ordered.

"After I told Coleman where to stick his bribe, I got a package in the mail. It was a burner phone. And it had a text on it, saying if I wanted Earnest to live, I would wipe his files, reply to the text to let them know it was done, then destroy the phone."

"When was this?"

"About a week and a half ago."

"How much time had passed from when you'd declined Coleman's offer?"

"Two or three days, I guess."

"Did you think the phone was from Coleman too?"

"No. It didn't seem like his style. He's the kind of guy who's all smiles and sunshine while he's secretly sizing you up, learning what makes you tick so he has power over you. That's how he became CEO, I suppose. But he likes to offer the carrot rather than the stick, you know? So you think giving him what he wants was your idea or at least feel like it was a win-win. He might blackmail someone, but threaten to kill them?"

"What convinced you the threat was real?"

I heard a long, indrawn breath.

"They sent me a"—his voice cracked—"finger. A human finger."

"Did you think it was Earnest's?"

"No. I mean, I rang him to check, and he was fine. But it convinced me they were serious."

"Why didn't you tell Earnest?"

"I did. He didn't care. It only made him more determined to keep doing what he was doing. But I couldn't let him do it. Die for the sake of exposing one more secret. It wasn't worth his life!" Jay started to sob. Great big messy choking sobs. "But they . . . killed him . . . anyway."

I felt like a monster listening to his grief. And guilty for thinking he might've betrayed Earnest for cash. I also felt bad for having such a short temper with him. He must have been tormenting himself over this, wondering what he should've done differently, and he'd have to shoulder this burden for the rest of his life.

Connor's voice held none of my sympathy. "Why didn't you tell us any of this earlier?"

Jay reined in his sobs. "Because I'd already wiped the files and I knew that'd make me look guilty. I'd gotten rid of the phone and everything before I found out Earnest was gone, so I had no proof at all. I didn't know what to do. I've been agonizing over it. Then when you came over here this morning, I saw a chance to put you onto Coleman in case I'm wrong about him being behind it. But what else could I do?"

I'm sure Connor would've had a few ideas, but he just said, "Tell me exactly what you did with the phone, the finger, and anything else you received with the threats."

"I followed their instructions with the phone before I heard he was dead. I smashed it to bits and chucked the pieces down a few different drainpipes."

If it weren't for this morning's rain, we might've been able to retrieve the pieces, but they could've been washed anywhere by now.

"And I knew I should've kept the . . . part . . . for evidence, but I couldn't stand having it in the house—"

"Did it smell bad?"

"No, it was the idea of it. I didn't want to sleep with it nearby. But I was too scared to go to the cops. I thought about dumping it in the trash, but that seemed wrong somehow, like, disrespectful to the person it once belonged to. So I posted it to the police in an unmarked envelope. I knew it was a long shot, but I hoped maybe they'd track down the guy behind it all."

"Good. One last question, Mr. Massey."

Jay and I waited a couple of beats to hear what it would be.

"Did you accept Coleman's bribe given you were being forced to erase the files anyway?"

Jay started sobbing again. "Yes. I did."

I WATCHED THE DARK FIGURE on the street walking toward me. Despite knowing it was probably Connor, I couldn't be sure in the shadows cast by the occasional streetlight, and I was feeling jumpy. My eyes stayed on the figure while my hand searched my bag for the Taser. A few seconds later and a dozen feet nearer, I released it and slumped back in my seat, reminding myself to breathe.

The finger thing had me freaked.

Was the person who smacked me over the head the same one who'd chopped off a person's finger?

As if he'd read my mind, Connor climbed into the

car and said, "I think it would be best if you stayed at my house again tonight."

"Okay," I said too quickly. I took a big breath. "If it's not all that much trouble, I mean?"

"It's the easiest way to keep you safe." He turned the engine over and pulled out onto the road.

"Well. I still have my Taser and pepper spray. And I held my own against Albert." Albert was a creep who'd dosed me with GHB-X, a potent derivative of the date-rape drug, and tried to seduce me. Twice. I'd tasered him and ran away as fast as I could. Then I'd hidden behind Etta and her Glock until the police came.

Connor glanced at me, and I saw from the set of his mouth that he was mad. Perhaps I shouldn't have brought up Albert. "Albert wasn't threatening physical violence," he said.

"Mr. Black was," I reminded him.

"Well, maybe I should've had you stay with me then too. But Mr. Black was paid to scare you. He wasn't going to kill you, and you knew what he looked like so you could be cautious. He also wasn't about to use Oliver or Meow against you. This person is an unknown. The few clues we have suggest they have no qualms mutilating bodies and could have already murdered Earnest."

In other words, scary as hell. "Okay. I just wanted to make sure. I feel bad about invading your home now that it's not a job requirement."

"Don't."

We stopped at a traffic light, and he looked over at me again. "I mean it. The truth is, I missed you. A little."

The light turned green, and my cheeks turned red. *Connor had missed me?* I couldn't believe it.

Even though we'd developed a camaraderie when we'd been forced to work together, it was a bond that came from being on the same side of a life-or-death investigation. On a personal level, I was under the distinct impression that he'd barely tolerated me.

Sure, there'd been some sexual attraction there after he'd had his stylist make me over to his tastes, and he might have slept with me if I'd been willing. But when we were trapped in the car together for two and half hours on our way to interview a suspect, he'd avoided conversation about everything but the case and tried to drug me so I'd sleep all the way home.

How could he miss my company?

I cleared my throat, but no words came to me. I didn't want to make a joking retort and laugh off the weightiness of this tiny yet big-feeling confession, but I also wasn't ready to say anything too, well, significant.

I cleared my throat again. "I guess I should admit that Etta wasn't the only one who missed having you around. I kind of missed that as well."

And I realized how true that was. I had missed his

strong, ever-competent presence and the opportunity to witness the brief glimpses of the man underneath. The flashes of humor, anger, amusement, and concern. Cuddling Meow on the couch while he waited for me. Trying to snap me out of it when I was overwhelmed with guilt and fear. Teaching me to use pepper spray on a Spider-Man cutout of all things. And the kiss. The one we'd shared in the elation of learning Dana was going to live.

I swallowed hard and let my mind drift along with the hum of the engine. Now I felt uncomfortable about sleeping at his house for a different reason.

Had I hoped some professional wall had been broken and I'd meet the person underneath Connor's mask, I would've been sadly disappointed. We drove the rest of the way to his Beverly Hills mansion in silence.

I wondered whether Connor was thinking about the kiss too.

The mundane matter of discussing dinner options coaxed us to speak again. Maria had left us a Tuscan roast tomato and white bean soup with the best garlic bread I'd ever tasted. I swiped the last piece and, emboldened by the food and the bottle of red accompanying it, asked, "So, what did you miss about me?"

Connor eyed the empty plate. "I missed you eating me out of house and home."

I made a show of devouring the buttery, caramelized, garlicky goodness and smacked my lips. "What else?"

"I missed testing your poison-detection abilities."

Shock rammed into me. I hadn't bothered to check properly. Had I overlooked something? I did a physical inventory. Heartbeat, temperature, throat, stomach, senses, and mental faculties all seemed normal. "Funny," I said.

By the light in his eyes, he must have agreed with my assessment. "I missed watching your nose wrinkle when you drank automatic drip coffee."

"Ugh. I still can't believe you deceived me so completely."

He absentmindedly swirled the wine in his glass. "I missed catching you staring at my ass."

My cheeks heated. "I don't know what you're talking about."

"I missed you stealing my underwear."

Dammit. After my triumph yesterday, I'd forgotten to replace the spare pair of undies in my bag. Which meant I was back to stealing Connor's. "Okay. I don't like this game after all. What's for dessert?"

The answer was dark chocolate brownie with homemade vanilla bean ice cream. After it was plated up, we fell back into our usual pattern of talking about the case.

"I'll bring Commander Hunt up to speed and see if he wants to interview Coleman with me or not," Connor said. "He might be able to track down that finger and tell us if the prints are in the system and whether the person it was removed from was dead or alive at the time."

"Surely it can't be hard for the police to find the finger that was posted to them?"

"You might be surprised how many body parts a police force the size of the LAPD get posted to them, but knowing when Mr. Massey sent it will help. The fact he said it didn't smell horrible suggests it was embalmed or very, very fresh."

I stopped eating and put down my spoon.

"Sorry."

"It's fine. I can afford to skip dessert." It was true. But watching that ice cream melt and go to waste felt sacrilegious.

"Even with the cash bribe to Massey, it will be hard to pin anything concrete on Coleman. Whether or not he put a hit on Earnest, he's good at playing dirty."

Connor was right, and I wasn't sure what to do about it. Coleman was out of my league.

"We also need to respond to that text message threat about the flash drive before whoever's behind it decides to escalate things."

Escalate things. That sounded bad. "Do you think Coleman's behind that too?"

"My gut says no. Like Massey said, the direct threats aren't his style, and there's no way he would've broken into Earnest's apartment himself. I think we're dealing with two players."

"So what do I say?"

"Just that you found it and destroyed it as instructed."

Another lie. I should be better at them by now. "What if they ask for proof?"

"Then we'll manufacture some. But like I said, there is no real proof you could provide even if you had the flash drive and videotaped yourself smashing it to pieces, because they have no way of telling if you copied it first. They have to be relying on fear. Like they did with Massey."

"Are we sure it's the same person?"

"No, but the basic MO is similar and their overt goal of destroying data is the same."

"But I didn't get a . . . finger." I shuddered even saying it.

Connor scooped up the last of his brownie and ice cream, unconcerned. "I don't think your part was planned in advance. They must have intended to find the flash drive themselves for some reason, only you interrupted their search."

"Then I guess it's good that they don't carry human fingers around in case of emergency."

Connor's lips did their twitch thing that was the equivalent of a smile by most people's standards. "Send the message, Avery."

I did as he said. "Now what?"

"We go to bed. You might as well sleep on the mattress in my room again since you didn't snore."

My eyes rushed to his, wondering whether there was any more meaning to his words.

"It will make it easier to protect you."

Somehow I didn't think his home would be easy to break into, but I followed him down the hallway anyway. On my bed there was a neatly folded pile: navy cotton pajamas, two pairs of briefs, and a brand new toothbrush.

"I had Maria pick up a few things for you. Seeing as you have a habit of requiring my protection."

I admit it. I was touched. Even if it did mean, like Levi had said, that they had every confidence in my ability to find trouble. "Thank you."

"No problem." He waited until my hand was on the door to the en-suite before adding, "But I'm going to miss seeing you in one of my T-shirts."

15

I FELT LIKE A KID having a sleepover as I settled into my bed with Connor a few yards away. It was kind of . . . cozy. Not a word I'd ever expected to associate with Connor, but somehow sleeping in one of his impersonal guest rooms would have left me wishing for my own rainbow-vomit bed. Here, knowing that he'd missed me, I felt snuggly and safe.

At least I did until my phone buzzed with a new text.

Describe the flash drive you destroyed.

Crap.

There was a silver lining though. Connor got up to read the message, so I finally saw what he liked to wear to bed. Just his gray trunks. I snorted when I realized they'd match his eyes. *Like I'd be looking at his eyes.*

The sight of his body, even in the low light of the lamp, gave me goosebumps. He was broad and muscular but with a lean, athletic build rather than that of a beefcake gym junkie. His strong shoulders and chest tapered to gently defined abs and . . . well, let's just say he was exquisitely sculpted in *every* way. He was flawlessly groomed too, which wasn't surprising given the clothed version I knew of him. I don't mind body hair, or I wouldn't have married an Italian, but the overall effect would forever inspire my fantasies.

If it wasn't for the message freaking me out, I might've been powerless to resist running my hands over him and pulling him into my bed.

Which would've been a mistake.

His admission that he'd missed me wasn't enough to stake a relationship on, and I wasn't interested in sex on the side. Or at least most of me wasn't interested in sex on the side. Some of me was extremely interested.

It took me a long time to get to sleep.

I peeked at him while he concentrated on his freshly toasted muesli across the table. He was fully clothed again, which was the best way for him to be for the sake of my self-control. I was also fully clothed and drinking my second espresso of the day, which was the best way for me to be.

We'd put off replying about the flash drive until this morning in order to buy us more time. Or at least give the person behind it less time. Connor thought they might be bluffing, so we made up a generic description and hoped it would convince them.

It was metallic silver.

There hadn't been a response, and I was crossing my fingers there wouldn't be one, except maybe: *Thanks ever so much. I'll stop threatening you now.*

"So did Police Commander Hunt decide he wanted to come along when you speak with Coleman?" I asked, mostly to get my mind off my anonymous menace.

"No. Said he's got better things to do."

"Like what? Patrolling the streets, scaring small children?"

Connor looked amused. "Something like that."

"Any news on the finger?"

"Also no. But it's still early."

Fabulous. I wondered which poor soul would have to spend their morning sorting through all the posted appendages to find it. "Do we have time to swing by my apartment to pick up some more clothes?"

"I took the liberty of having my stylist purchase a few items for you."

"What?" This was not the reprieve it should've been for someone who hated shopping. His stylist and I had very different priorities around fashion and practicality. At least Maria had picked a comfy pair of pajamas for me. "Why?"

"I thought it best for you not to potentially run into

the press wearing the same clothes as yesterday after not being home again all evening."

Good point.

"And she remembered all your sizes and color palette."

That was less good. It would have been more useful if I was the same size.

Connor must have seen the dread on my face. "I told her to choose more comfortable, casual options for you, now that it's not a matter of my hypothetical reputation."

When he'd first interviewed me for the position of his Shade, it was his reputation he'd cited as the reason I needed a makeover. *A big one*, he'd specified. It had done wonders for my ego.

"Thanks," I said, wondering what it meant that he'd requested more casual options for me this time around. No hot-blooded male could prefer this version of me to the stylist-designed one. So maybe his choice was for my benefit. Or maybe he was tactfully calling me fat.

Then again, Connor was anything but tactful.

An hour and a half later, I was sitting in the SUV again. Dudley's drool had miraculously disappeared from the back door panels, and I was wearing stretchy form-hugging pants, an oversized forest-green knit jumper that fell midthigh, and non-waterlogged ankle boots. The pants fit suspiciously well. Connor must have told his stylist I'd gained weight.

I was both grateful and depressed.

Connor was in the Aptech building, his audio recording in my ear.

"Mr. Stiles. What did I do to deserve another face-to-face with your friendly self?" Coleman asked. His voice was even more slick today if that were possible.

"Lie. Bribe. Cheat. Kill," Connor said. "Shall I go on?"

"Well I do love a good story, but why don't you sit down first? It sounds like this could be a long one."

From what I could hear, Connor didn't sit.

"We know you paid Jay Massey a hundred grand cash to wipe Earnest Dunst's hard drives."

"Interesting, interesting. That's the funny thing about cash, isn't it? So hard to trace, and personal testimonies are so unreliable. Especially from the person who committed the criminal act. Go on, what else do you have for me?"

"You remember our conversation about getting the press involved? I don't need Mr. Massey's testimony to stand up in court. I just need to let a few reporters know about it. That kind of thing can take an awful long time to sort out. And you have the revolutionary Pearl operating system going live in two months. People are saying its success will make or break your company. Why don't you tell me what you have for me."

"Nicely maneuvered, Mr. Stiles. It's not often I come across a challenging opponent, and I appreciate the entertainment, so let me tell you a little story in return." There was a quiet shuffling noise before he continued. "Cigar? Ah well, you won't mind if I have one myself."

A chair creaked, and I imagined Coleman leaning back, feet on his desk. Probably his feet were on the ground.

"Let's say, hypothetically, that I discovered there was a leak in my company. That an inside man was giving away confidential—entirely legal, of course—information away to a third party. Hypothetically, I might pay someone to delete all record of this information, and at the same time, put a plan in place to deal with the leak."

"How would you do that?"

"Hypothetically?"

Connor grunted.

Coleman sounded like he was enjoying himself. "Let's say there were three people who knew enough to be the leak. I might approach each of them individually and tell them I'm planning on retiring next year and have chosen them to step up and take over the company. Of course I can't make a formal announcement until we launch the Pearl operating system. Wouldn't want to shake consumer or investor confidence and all that, but I wanted to give them a heads-up anyway."

There was a pause, and I wondered if he was blowing smoke rings or something. Or maybe he'd grown a strawberry blond mustache since the photo I'd seen of him was taken, and he was twiddling it.

"Wouldn't you say that the individual who'd leaked the information would then be extremely interested in containing it?" he asked.

"Not if they leaked the information in good conscience to stop an injustice or to protect people from being taken advantage of," Connor said.

"I assure you, Mr. Stiles, none of these individuals have a conscience."

I made a mental note to never use any of their products. Unless they really did design a phone operating system that could pick up dog poop.

"The beauty of my strategy is that I would also, by way of monitoring the three, find out who the leak had been in the first place. So you can see I had my bases covered, with no need to resort to such rudimentary methods as murder."

"How did you know you had a leak?" Connor asked.

"Ah. Now that would be telling." The chair creaked again. "If that's all I can help you with today, I have important things to go on with. Leaks to find. Products to launch. All that sort of thing."

"Give me the names, Coleman. Of the suspected leaks."

"Why would I do that?"

"To humor me, of course. So I leave you to your important things."

I could hear the silent threat and was sure Coleman wouldn't miss it either: *So I don't bring you up on charges of conspiracy or obstruction of justice in a homicide investigation or have the press drag your name through the muck.*

"All right. To humor you."

16

CONNOR RETURNED WITH A LIST of names. Jamison, McCarthy, and Daubney.

"What's next?" I asked.

"We find out what each of Coleman's suspected leaks were doing when Earnest's apartment was broken into."

"You mean when I got hit on the head?"

"Yes. Many people won't have a solid alibi for one thirty to three in the middle of the night when Earnest was killed, but there's a good chance they'll have one around lunchtime. And Coleman's given us a strong motive for someone on this list to eliminate Dunst, threaten Massey, and be hell-bent on finding that flash drive."

"Will you put the research team onto it?"

"No. I want to get a handle on each suspect. To look them in the eye and see if they're the type who could chop off someone's finger and pop it in the mail."

Connor pulled over suddenly. "That's Ms. McCarthy."

Coleman had identified her as his personal assistant and one of the potential leaks. Her name seemed familiar, and I was pretty sure she was the woman who'd wished Connor a wonderful Christmas the first time we'd come to Aptech.

Trusting the dark, tinted windows to hide me enough that I wouldn't be recognized, I watched as Connor exited the SUV and made his way toward her.

Ms. McCarthy was bustling down the street with two large coffees and a heavy pile of dry cleaning over her shoulder. At five foot one in inch-high heels, she was dwarfed by the dry-cleaning bags, and her petite hands made the jumbo takeout cups look cartoonish.

I hoped she wasn't the one responsible for knocking me out cold and forcing me to sleep at Connor's for protection. I'd never live it down.

"Ms. McCarthy, we met yesterday. I'm a consultant with the LAPD, and I need to talk to you about an ongoing investigation."

She was unmoved by Connor's credentials. Or his striking good looks. "Will this take long?"

"Hopefully not. I have one question for you. Where were you on Sunday afternoon between twelve thirty and one?"

"I was working, so I would've been on my lunch break. I usually pack myself a salad and go to Crescent Park to eat it."

That explained why she was so snotty. Working Sundays with salad for lunch wouldn't cheer anyone up.

"Did someone see you?"

"Probably. There are always people about, but I don't know any of them personally and couldn't say who was or wasn't there that day. However, if you've got nothing better to do, you're welcome to go and ask."

"Thank you for your permission. One more thing."

She glared at him. "You said you only had one question."

"I lied. But this is the last of them. Can you tell me where to find Mr. Daubney and Mr. Jamison?"

"How should I know?"

"Because I'm willing to bet you know everything that's going on at Aptech."

Her glare subsided, just a bit. "All right. Daubney is in New York closing a deal, and Jamison keeps his own hours but is usually at Fitness First gym between eight and nine. On Lincoln Boulevard. Now if you'll excuse me, I really must get back to the office."

She didn't wish him a wonderful Christmas this time. Instead, she hoisted the dry cleaning higher to stop it dragging and sped past Connor like there was a pack of mangy males hot on her heels.

"So what did her eyes tell you?" I asked Connor when he climbed into the car.

"That if I didn't let her get back to the office, she'd stab me with one of her stilettos, wrap me up in the dry cleaning, and toss me into the nearest dumpster."

Fifteen minutes later, I was still sitting in the SUV while Connor entered Fitness First gym. From what I could see of the place through the floor-to-ceiling glass windows, they should've called it Indulgence First. There seemed to be more people lounging on daybeds around the pool than in it, and attractive waiters and waitresses flitted between them serving drinks.

Suspected leak number two was Mr. Jamison, Aptech's development manager. I wouldn't be meeting the man in the flesh, but I did have a photo the research team had sent over just now.

Jamison was the type you'd pass on the streets and never remember seeing. Thick caterpillar eyebrows crawled over deep-set blue eyes in a mild round face. A pair of rimless spectacles perched on his nondescript nose, and a half-hearted smile adorned his lips, telling me he was harmless. I was unconvinced.

I heard doors swish open and then the whirring, beeping, pounding, and puffing noises of a gym as Connor tried to locate Jamison. So maybe some people were exercising.

A few minutes later Connor introduced himself. “What were your whereabouts on Sunday between twelve thirty and one p.m.?”

There was a moment’s pause. “Can I ask what this investigation is about?” I noticed Mr. Jamison wasn’t breathing hard. Either he was super fit or was one of the people lazing around the pool.

“I’m not at liberty to discuss it,” Connor said. “And if I were, it wouldn’t change your answer, would it?”

“Of course not. But curiosity is a valuable human trait and one that matters in my line of work. Curiosity leads to exploration and exploration leads to innovation, so you can see it’s natural I would ask.”

“Please answer my question.”

“Certainly. Let me check my calendar.” Another pause. “Sunday wasn’t it? What time did you say?”

“Between twelve thirty and one,” Connor said, sounding irritated.

“It seems I was in a meeting with Kyle and York Development.”

Didn’t anyone in the tech industry take weekends off?

“Where was this?”

“Their headquarters in Venice.” I presumed he meant Venice in Westside LA rather than Italy, but I could’ve been mistaken.

“How many people can confirm that you were there?”

"At least three, but I'd prefer you don't follow this up unless it's strictly necessary. I wouldn't want them to get the impression that the police are investigating Aptech for anything."

"Thanks for your time, Mr. Jamison."

Connor joined me in the SUV after some more beeping, thumping, and puffing noises.

"What did his eyes tell you?" I asked.

"That he's not nearly so banal or pleasant as he likes to appear. I'm starting to think Coleman only hires sociopaths."

"Maybe it's part of the recruitment selection criteria. He did assure you that none of them have a conscience."

"I was hoping he was wrong. If he's right about that, then he's also right that he wouldn't have to worry about the leak. As long as he managed to convince each person that he was sincere in choosing them to take over anyway."

Which implied that whatever Coleman was up to, he had a good chance of getting off scot-free. "What do we do now?"

"The research team has verified that the CFO, Mr. Daubney, is where he's supposed to be in New York, and his flights and hotel corroborate that he arrived Saturday and ordered room service around the time you were attacked on Sunday."

"One ruled out, two to go." If our theory was correct, it meant I'd been knocked out by someone with caterpillar eyebrows or a pint-sized grump. I wasn't sure which was worse.

"Yes. We have to confirm Jamison's and McCarthy's alibis and run a background check on the pair of them, but I'll delegate that to the team. Even if their alibis don't hold up, we need more evidence. I'm going to update Hunt and see if I can expedite the identification of that finger."

"What should I do?"

"That's up to you. But it's been at least an hour since we ate, so I'm sure you must be starving."

IT HAD BEEN AT LEAST *two* hours since I'd eaten, but I was trying to lose weight, so I left Connor to deal with Hunt and caught an Uber ride to Mrs. Dunst's house. She embraced me. "Isobel, darling, come on in." The phone rang in the hall as we entered, but she made no move to answer it. Instead, she asked, "Have the reporters been harassing you too?"

"A little," I admitted. Actually, I'd had more calls in the past twenty-four hours than the entire year prior.

"What's the world coming to? Don't they have better things to do? I've got a right mind to disconnect the phone altogether."

"It's because of Earnest's website. I know he never tried to convince you otherwise, but it was very well respected. He's practically a celebrity in some circles, and they want to know what happened to him. They care about what happened to him."

"They have a funny way of showing it."

"Well, it might not be the reporters themselves that care," I amended, "but they're only so persistent because there are lots of people who do. Otherwise it wouldn't be such a big story." I dumped my bag on her dining table and put the kettle on.

Mrs. Dunst moved to the cupboard to get tea bags and sugar. Maybe she'd noticed me sizing up her grinning squirrel canister.

"I suppose you're right," she said. "I hadn't looked at it that way."

I found some cups, took the tea things from her, and gave her another hug. I still felt like a fraud, but her need was painfully obvious and I hoped I could use my fraudulent position to do some good.

"How are you holding up?" I asked.

"Okay, I guess. I'm so lost without him that it's hard to even know the answer to that. Everyone's been lovely to me, and I'm overwhelmed by their support. I just wish the police had caught the son of the bitch who did this to my Earnest before we bury him tomorrow. I have a feeling he'd rest easier that way, if you know what I mean?"

"Yeah, I do," I said. "He spent his life seeking out justice. It seems like he should get his."

We moved to the dining table and sipped our tea in comfortable silence for a while.

"Can I give you a casserole?" Mrs. Dunst asked. "People keep dropping them off, which I appreciate, but I'm not hungry. They don't seem to understand that grieving saps your appetite and eating is the last thing I feel like doing."

"Why don't you freeze it? It's fair enough if you don't feel like eating, but you probably won't feel like cooking for a while either." It was a shame my grief didn't affect me the same way. Instead, I kept craving comfort food.

She got up and opened the freezer door. Every inch was filled with neatly packed containers. "Seriously, Izzy, I have more casseroles here than I could consume in a decade. Please take one. Or two. Or five. I don't want them to go to waste, but if I have to eat them all, I'll go mad." She looked at me helplessly.

"Okay. I'll take some," I relented. Then, thinking of the comfort food thing, I asked, "Is there anything that you do feel like eating?"

She shook her head.

"Not even ice cream? Or cookies? I make some mean cookies."

"I guess I might eat some cookies."

"Then I'll bake you some and bring them over soon."

A small smile crept its way across her face. "Only if you swap them for more casseroles."

I laughed. "We have a deal."

A few hours later, I caught another Uber ride home. Thanks to my former years as a barista, I was able to balance the two casserole trays in one hand as I crossed the landing, digging for my key. There was a small package waiting by the door, wrapped in Christmas paper. I put the trays down to inspect it, wondering if it might be from Etta or even my family in Australia. But there were no postage marks or stamps, just my name scrawled in black marker.

Curiosity piqued, I slid a finger under the tape and unwrapped a small jewelry box. Who would be gifting me jewelry? Surely not Connor? Or Levi? I flipped the lid open. And screamed.

Footsteps pounded toward me, but I couldn't take my eyes off it. The human thumb.

"What's wrong?" The voice was Etta's. She sucked in a breath. "Oh."

She must be staring at the thumb now too.

"What does the note say?"

I hadn't even seen a note. But she was right. It was pinned to the inside of the lid.

Don't lie about the flash drive again.

"Are you okay, dear? You look a little pale. Maybe you should sit down."

"Um." The jewelry box shook. Oh. It was me doing the shaking.

"Let me see." That voice was not Etta's. It was a deep rumble. Like Mr. Black's.

A giant hand took the box from me. I surrendered it with relief, and the spell binding my eyes to it broke. Which allowed me to see Mr. Black looming over me. That was almost as scary.

"At least it's been preserved," he commented. He was wearing one of the white shirts he favored and dark blue jeans. I figured white shirts could be bleached to remove the bloodstains.

Except according to him, he was scared of blood.

His alleged fear didn't extend to severed body parts. He was examining the thumb carefully. To be fair, I hadn't noticed any blood on it.

"Looks like it was removed from someone already dead," he said, snapping the box shut. "I'd say they were embalmed first."

I didn't want to know how he could be so confident about it.

His gaze fell on me like a heavy blanket. With cement

blocks attached. "Do you owe money to somebody else?"

I concentrated on taking breaths. In. Out. In. Out. Nice and slow.

"Let's get her inside." That was Etta again. "Is there anyone I should call for you?"

In. Out. At least I couldn't see the thumb anymore.

Etta unlocked the door and ushered me into the apartment. "Give me your phone."

I handed it over.

"Connor? It's Etta here. I'm calling about Izzy. She's uh, found a human appendage on her doorstep. You might want to come over."

17

MR. BLACK MADE me an unexpectedly good cup of tea before excusing himself. He didn't want to be here if the police came. Again I tried not to think about that too much.

Etta walked him out. She'd once told me she chose an upstairs apartment because her doctor said as long as she could walk up a flight of stairs, she was healthy enough to keep having sex. She'd also pointed out that she could walk up and down them multiple times a day. Now whenever she escorted an attractive man out to his car, I couldn't help but remember her story.

"You're looking better," she told me when she returned. "Got some color back in your face. What should I do with these casseroles?"

"In the fridge is fine, thanks," I said, unable to envisage ever eating again. Be careful what you wish for. I'd washed my hands half a dozen times, but they didn't feel clean yet.

Maybe this was the beginning of a brilliant new weight-loss program. Send people severed appendages to look at whenever they felt hungry. It made me wonder where McCarthy or Jamison got their supply of severed fingers from.

Connor arrived with Commander Hunt, both wearing grim expressions. I couldn't tell if the grim thing was because of the human body part they'd come to collect or Oliver's poster on the door.

"Where is it?" Connor asked me.

"Right here, gentleman," Etta said with a flourish like she was on a game show pointing out their prize. "As you can see, it's been preserved and removed neatly postmortem." Now she was listing the prize's features. Or showing off her borrowed knowledge for Connor and Hunt's benefit.

"Very good," Hunt said, studying her with interest.

She preened under his gaze. How peculiar. Usually she went for men at least twenty years younger than her. Hunt was only about five.

"Could be from the same body," Connor said. *His* attention was still on the finger. "Male, white-collar worker with a similar skin tone."

Hunt forced his eyes back to the thumb. "Yes. It'll be easy enough to check. The finger pad is intact."

I bit my tongue to keep from asking if he'd figured out whom the first one was from. I wasn't supposed to know anything about the first one.

"Can we find out how it was delivered?" Hunt asked. "I don't suppose this building has surveillance?"

"No," said Etta and Connor at the same time.

"I normally might have noticed," Etta continued, "but I was out all morning while the painters finished in my apartment, and Oliver, that's Izzy's housemate, wasn't home either."

"Okay. I'll have uniforms ask around, see if anyone saw anything. In the meantime, I'm going to talk to Langley down at the station if you want to be there, Stiles."

Connor's face was impassive, as usual. "I'll meet you there."

"I'll walk you out, Police Commander," Etta said.

Yep, there she went, up and down the stairs again.

I watched them leave together, Hunt's stride deceptively slow and casual, with the coiled readiness of a predator, Etta's light and quick.

Maybe Etta was like one of those tiny birds that flitted around the predator's jaws to prove they could.

Connor's gaze landed on me as soon as they cleared the door, and his mask relaxed a fraction. "Are you all right?"

"Sure. Better than being poisoned or shot or knocked out anyway." I tried for a smile.

He sat down beside me. Close enough that his leg rested reassuringly against mine. "I'm not convinced losing a client or being threatened with human body parts is better. Just different. You're allowed to not be okay."

Tears pricked my eyes, but now wasn't the time to let them fall. "What's going on? Who's Langley?"

"We got lucky. The prints from the first finger were in the system. They belonged to a recently deceased government worker. The dead are normally removed from the database, but thanks to a backlog, his hadn't been processed yet. Another week, and they might have gotten away with it."

"I don't understand."

"The body the finger came from was donated to a medical science and education program. His cadaver was sent to a local university for medical students to learn on and was then supposed to be cremated. According to the university's records, he *was* cremated. Langley was the person responsible for cremating him."

My mind reeled. "Oh, wow."

"Want to come and listen in on the interview?"

Hunt had driven away, which left the coast clear for me to leave with Connor. Even so, I paused when we met Etta on the landing. "Isn't Hunt too old for you?"

She swatted my shoulder. “This is how you repay me for giving Connor a chance to comfort you? Pfft. Young people these days.”

“He’s very good-looking for an old coot,” I said, unswayed. “If you like the scary type. Which I know for a fact that you do.”

“Haven’t you got better things to do than harass me?”

“Are you blushing?” I countered. She wasn’t, but I knew she hated it on the rare occasions she did.

“Of course not.” Her cheeks tinged with the slightest hint of pink.

I grinned. “Enjoy the rest of your day.”

My grin faded as I hurried to catch up to Connor. That thumb was going to haunt my thoughts for a long time. Once we were both inside the cool leather interior of the SUV, Connor must have sensed my mood. “Would it cheer you up if I allow you to interrogate me?” he asked.

I stared at him, unsure if he was joking. He drove straight-backed in his navy dress shirt and black jeans, one arm on the wheel, the other resting on the stick shift. Calm. Competent. Compelling. The profile view of him was as appealing as the front, accentuating the perfect proportions of his features and the angle of his square jaw. His lashes and lips adding a touch of softness to the otherwise stern face.

"Will you answer questions on topics other than your bedroom prowess?" I asked, testing out his invitation.

He glanced over, and his expression was definitely warmer than normal. "Is there anything you'd prefer to learn?"

The words hung in the air like a challenge.

"Tell me about your family," I said at last. The answer to that ought to be illuminating. I doubted I'd get many questions, so I had to make sure they were well spent.

He muttered something that sounded like "straight for the throat" and drummed his fingers on the steering wheel before answering.

I counted his fingers to make sure they were all still attached.

"My mom was a PI in her heyday. Retired now, which means she has far too much time to scheme against my sister and me. She met my dad when she was paid to investigate him. He was a foot soldier in the 24th Infantry Division and died in the Gulf War when I was ten."

"Sorry."

He shrugged. "It happens. Especially to infantry."

There was no way he could feel so casual about it, but I was amazed he'd opened up at all. I wasn't going to push.

"Mom was incredibly strong. Didn't let us see her grieve much. She raised us alone and taught us the basics of PI work. We used to help her on simple surveillance jobs after school. I took to it, obviously. My sister became a mechanic."

"What's she like? Your sister?" His tone had lifted when he mentioned her.

"Cheerful. Lighthearted. She always tells me I'm stuffy."

I sniggered.

"She's exasperating too. Kind of like someone else I know." His eyes flicked my way. "You get one more question."

"Have you ever been married?"

"No."

"Care to elaborate?"

"No."

And that was that. His distraction had worked. The tantalizing glimpse into his life had given me a much-needed break from the case.

If I hadn't owed every penny I earned to a loan shark, I would have paid good money to meet his family.

18

CONNOR DROVE past the police station and found a space to leave the SUV a block and a half away. I touched his arm before he got out. "Thank you." His opening up had meant a lot to me, and I wanted him to know I didn't take it for granted.

He gave me a nod.

As my mind returned to the case and I waited for the interview to start, I wondered whether Hunt would find it suspicious that Connor had opted not to use the parking lot. With any luck, he'd stay inside and not even have the chance to notice.

"Mrs. Langley, I'm Police Commander Hunt and this is Mr. Stiles, a consultant on this case. Do you know why you're here today?"

"No?" The voice was high and nervous. Normal. Not like all the sociopaths in this investigation.

"You're responsible for cremating the cadavers donated to your university, correct?"

"That's right." I imagined her licking her lips.

"Then how is it that I have two severed parts of one of those cadavers in my evidence room?"

"I don't know."

"Are you sure about that? Because either way, you're going to lose your job, but if you're lying to me, you're looking at criminal charges for selling human body parts and obstruction of justice in a homicide investigation."

"Homicide?" she squeaked.

"Do you want to help a murderer, Mrs. Langley?"

"No. I . . ."

"If you tell us what you know, I'll speak to the DA for you, ask them to go easy given you're a first-time offender."

I counted to one before she caved.

"She made me do it. I had no choice."

"Who made you do it?"

"Ellen McCarthy. She knew I cheated on my husband." Langley started sobbing. "It was just once. Years ago when we were all in college. But she threatened to tell him if I didn't give her what she wanted."

"What did she want?"

"Five fingers. She didn't say what for. And I didn't sell them to her. I would never do that! But I had to save my marriage. I didn't have a choice."

I felt sickened. First Jay and now Langley. McCarthy was good at making people feel like they didn't have a choice. She really would be a suitable protégée for Coleman.

Hours later, Connor and Hunt were in the interrogation room again, and I was in the SUV with a cramp in my ass. Even so, I was happy to be sitting this one out. I couldn't believe that McCarthy, the five-foot midget, had sent me flying then knocked me cold. That this was whom Jay and I had been scared of. Who I was still scared of. What kind of person gift wrapped fingers? I'd never be able to look at a Christmas present the same way again.

And that wasn't even McCarthy's worst offense. All the evidence pointed toward her being Earnest's murderer. For some reason she'd chosen to leak him information, then changed her mind and done what was needed to silence him forever.

How was it possible to extinguish a life so casually? And how the hell did she manhandle him into the abandoned building?

"Ms. McCarthy, you seem like a smart woman," Hunt began, "so you must know how bad this looks for you.

Right now we have people searching your home and office, and I'm guessing they're going to find the burner phone you used to threaten Ms. Avery and hair that matches the one we retrieved from the scene of her assault. Even if they don't, we have your friend Langley's testimony that she provided you with the severed fingers that were delivered to Mr. Massey and Ms. Avery. And Massey's testimony that you threatened Earnest Dunst's life a few days before he was murdered."

"I didn't kill him." McCarthy said the words calmly.

Hunt's tone was dry. "You'll forgive me if I don't take you at your word."

"Look, I might've made threats, but that's all they were."

"Most empty threats don't involve human body parts, Ms. McCarthy."

"That's exactly why they involved body parts," she countered. "I've observed Coleman for years, and in that time I've learned that power is all about belief. If you can make someone believe what you want, then you can make someone do what you want. Coleman likes to learn all about his opponents so he can exploit their innate beliefs, weaknesses, and temptations, but I didn't have the time or knowledge to use that finesse here, so I made a small gesture to ensure they believed the threat was real. You should be applauding my method. It's much less crude than killing people."

"We'll be sure to give you a prison cell with a view. If you didn't murder Mr. Dunst. Why don't you start from the beginning?"

"You haven't scared me, gentlemen. I'll tell you my story because it's in my best interests to, not because of your intimidation tactics."

"Then we'd appreciate it if you got on with it."

Someone, and I was betting that someone was Ms. McCarthy, huffed.

"I've spent nine years of my life slaving away for Coleman. Organizing his schedule, writing his emails, everything but powdering his ass. I'm the one who does all the hard research so he can look superior and have the edge in meetings. But he's always acted like his success has been achieved in a vacuum and hardly acknowledged my existence, except as some convenient AI machine made to serve him. For all his insight into his opponents, he never took the time to assess me. I was sick to death of it all. So while he rubbed his hands in glee over his next dirty endeavor, I handed Earnest the keys to destroy him and stood back to watch his kingdom fall."

Wow. She had a flair for the dramatic. Maybe I should've guessed that from the fingers.

"How did you know Earnest?" Hunt asked.

"I knew him from when he used to work for Aptech, and I'd kept tabs on him since. I do it for everyone

Coleman has a connection to. So I knew about Earnest's whistle-blowing website, and it seemed like an excellent way to give Coleman the blow to his ego he needed. I might've helped him rise from the ashes, or I might've let him stay down. I hadn't decided yet. But then a bit over a week and a half ago he acknowledged me. Told me he was aware I all but ran the place and he'd chosen me to take over the company when he planned to retire at the end of next year. So I had to get the keys back."

"What's the company worth?" Hunt asked.

"Three hundred million."

"That sounds to me like ample motive for murder."

"I didn't need to murder him. I just had to get rid of the files. It wouldn't matter what Earnest knew if he had no proof. He was far too scrupulous to make a claim without ensuring he could prove it beyond all reasonable doubt. That's why he hadn't published the article on Aptech already. He wanted to triple-check and verify everything I'd given him."

"Then why did you tell Jay Massey that Earnest would die if he didn't delete the hard drives?"

"Because from what I knew of Jay, it was what would motivate him the most. He loved Earnest. I didn't think he'd be bribed to act against him, and he might hesitate to do it for his own safety, but how could he balk at saving the life of his dearest friend?" There was a quiet pause. "Oh stop looking at me like that. If I'd known Earnest was going to get himself murdered, I would've come up with a different threat so I wasn't implicated, wouldn't I?"

"Why not have Massey destroy the flash drive too?"

"Because I'd given Earnest the flash drive myself, and unlike his computer, the only information on it was what I was trying to contain. It pointed too directly to me, and I couldn't trust that Jay wouldn't look at it and figure it out. I was organizing a meeting with Earnest to get it back myself, but he died before it happened."

Probably the phone call I remembered Earnest taking. The one from the burner phone.

"Which is why you were searching his apartment before you were interrupted by Ms. Avery."

"Yes. I knew after she reported the break-in that I wouldn't be able to go near the apartment again, so I had to motivate her to deal with it for me. Except she destroyed the wrong flash drive. Stupid fool."

I puffed up in indignation, but no one could see or hear me. I'd have to make do with visualizing her itty-bitty ass in jail.

"What was on the flash drive?"

"You don't know?" Triumph rang in her voice. "You haven't located it yet, have you? Ah, well that's excellent news, thank you."

"I recollect you agreed to cooperate, Ms. McCarthy."

"And I am. As far as it pertains to your murder investigation. In fact, I think that covers everything I have to say, so we can wrap it up here, or you can call my attorney."

"Nothing you've said has proven your innocence, so it would be in your best interest to give us another lead. Do you have any idea who might've wanted Earnest dead?"

She huffed again. "Oh come on. He was a stubborn, wealthy perfectionist with agoraphobia, a drug history, and a website that toppled powerful people to financial ruin or worse. You can't tell me you're hurting for leads?"

MCCARTHY WAS RIGHT. We shouldn't have been hurting for leads, but the deleted data and the flash drive had seemed too coincidental to not be related to Earnest's death, so we'd followed them as far as they went. And it turned out, they were related to his death, but apparently they weren't the cause of it.

Jay wouldn't have deleted Earnest's hard drives if he hadn't gone missing, leaving his apartment unoccupied. McCarthy wouldn't have broken into his apartment to retrieve the flash drive had he been alive to meet with. But what she'd said was true. Earnest would never have published the story without the evidence to back it. So if no one had killed him to stop his latest story coming out, who had, and why?

The sun had set long ago, so I sat in the dark while Hunt and Connor wrapped up the interview and pressed charges against Ms. McCarthy. Even though I was waiting for him, I started when Connor unlocked the door. One look at his face told me his mood was as black as mine. He rested a moment before sliding the key into the ignition.

Someone tapped on my window. With the interior light on, I couldn't see who. I hesitated until Connor gave me a nod, then I rolled it down.

Fear thrummed through my veins when I recognized the figure.

"Ms. Avery."

I swallowed hard.

"I thought I told you to stay the hell out of my case."

"I have been. I was just—"

"I recognize the receiving end of a wire when I see one. Step out of the car."

I opened the door and climbed out, my movements jerky with trepidation. Hunt watched on with the menace of a wounded grizzly.

Connor got out too and stepped in between us. "This is a little over the top, Commander—"

"Stand down, Stiles. You should know better than to bring her into this." He snapped the cuffs on, and the reality of the situation hit me. As shocking and inescapable as the cold metal biting into my wrists. I was going to jail. Me. The closest I'd ever come to it before was that unpaid parking ticket that I'd lost in the mess of my bag once.

Connor wasn't standing down. He was standing in Hunt's way.

It didn't matter. Hunt shouldered past him with enough force to push Connor back a step. "You're lucky I don't toss your ass in jail too," he snarled, dragging me behind him.

Oh my gosh. I was really going to jail. My mouth opened and shut, trying to find words that would turn the situation around. But Hunt was unstoppable. Impenetrable. Criminal bruiser-for-hire, Mr. Black, was easier to reason with. There seemed something wrong about that.

"What are you charging her with?" Connor asked, striding after us.

"Nothing yet, but keep asking and I'll write up a long list."

That convinced Connor to stop.

Hunt marched me down the dark street without a word, then into the bright lights of the police station. The same station I'd walked through a few days ago, only now the few faces that looked my way held different expressions.

A tear leaked out of one eye, and humiliatingly, I couldn't even brush it away as Hunt was still dragging me along by my cuffed hands. I shook my hair forward to cover my face and walked on. This time we didn't stop at the interrogation box. We stopped in a long, narrow room that was in sore need of a new coat of paint.

I was looking at the paint to avoid looking at the barred row of cells.

It didn't prevent the cells' occupants from looking at me.

"Yoo-hoo!"

"What you in for?"

"I bet she's a ho."

The lucky policeman on jail duty stood up. "All right, enough."

The comments didn't stop, but they did lower in volume.

"You can leave all your personal effects with Martinez here," Hunt told me. "That includes your jewelry and anything in your pockets."

Martinez looked bored. I supposed it was better than looking too interested in my possessions. My bag was in Connor's car, so there wasn't much. My phone, candy cane earrings, a king-size Caramello wrapper, and a clump of lint. Martinez scrawled each item on a receipt.

"I don't need those back," I said, pointing at the wrapper and lint.

"We'll return them to you, ma'am. Don't want any misunderstandings later."

Fabulous.

Hunt patted me down with methodical indifference, and I tried to convince myself it was like going to the doctor. Or a full-body masseuse. He gave a nod to Martinez. Surprise, surprise, I didn't have any weapons hidden on my person.

"Fill in your details here, check over the list of your personal effects, then sign your name at the bottom."

I suppressed a sigh and leaned over the form. In all the stories you hear about prison, nobody tells you about the paperwork.

Maybe I was supposed to be flattered they trusted me to wield something as dangerous as a pen.

When I was done, Hunt prodded me toward the cell block. I suspected he'd usually hand the mundane business of processing a perp to somebody else. Which must mean he was relishing throwing my ass in jail too much to give it up.

It was then I realized that while the dividing walls between the cells were solid brick, each cell was set up for two. Adrenaline flowed through my veins. What type of criminal would I be sharing with? A drug dealer? A murderer? McCarthy?

Please don't let it be McCarthy.

Hunt shoved me inside the nearest cell and locked it behind me. "Sleep tight, Avery."

All I could tell about my cellmate was that they were large and fast asleep. They were covered head to toe in a gray blanket, but I knew the fast asleep thing by the guttural snores bouncing off the brick walls.

At least it couldn't be McCarthy. She was tiny and too much of a control freak to snore.

Grateful to postpone facing them, whoever they were, I went to the unoccupied bunk and curled up on it, feeling vulnerable and exposed. Bunk was a generous term for the fixed metal platform with a gym mat on top. I pulled the scratchy blanket over me and wondered how the hell it had come to this.

I'd only been trying to help. And for what? Our most promising theory was a dead end, so my inside knowledge had done nothing but lead us on a wild goose chase. Or a wild sociopath chase. We hadn't even figured out what Earnest had been planning to expose.

A few more tears leaked out, and I brushed them away. His funeral was tomorrow morning. Would Hunt allow me to go? Mrs. Dunst wouldn't understand if I was a no-show, and while I hated feeling like a fraud, I hated the idea of her going without moral support even more.

My pity party wasn't helping anyone. I closed my eyes against the harsh, unfeeling glare of the fluorescent lights and tried to escape in sleep.

19

TWO HOURS INTO my attempt at sleep, the on-duty police officer rapped on the bars. "Avery? You missed the dinner round, but you can have a bottle of water if you want it."

I got up, mostly to stretch out my stiff limbs, and took the water. Would I get food, too, if I said I was a diabetic? The officer moved on before I decided whether it was worth the risk of being caught out.

There was a piece of paper stuck to the bottom of the bottle. I flipped it upside down.

Don't worry. I'll get you out.

Connor. It must be. I felt a rush of gratitude toward him. I had no idea how he'd managed to get the note to me, but the gesture meant a lot. And surely if he could orchestrate the note, he could arrange my freedom too.

I crawled back onto the gym mat and, with the piece of paper clutched in my hand, found a piece of hope to clutch in my heart.

The note helped me get through the next eight hours, but sleep was far from the escape I was hoping for. On the bright side, pretending to doze did stop me having to talk to my cellmate when she eventually stopped snoring.

Unfortunately, ten hours into my incarceration, I was busting for the toilet. Even more unfortunate, the toilet was affixed to the wall between our bunks, with no privacy at all.

Except for a one-night stand that convinced me never to do another one-night stand, my doodah hadn't been bared in front of anyone since my ex-husband. I wasn't keen on baring it now.

But not even Connor could save me from my bladder.

When I couldn't hold on any longer, my cellmate took my emergence from the itchy blanket as an invitation to talk. She was big and black and beautiful and sat on her bunk like it was a sofa in the finest luxury hotel. "Hell, girl, what're you looking so sad for?"

I finished my business and returned to my bunk. I didn't want to talk about it.

"Did your man beat you? You 'bout to do hard time? Your friend got shot? What?"

When she put it that way, maybe my issues weren't so bad. "I'm worried I'll miss a funeral," I told her. It was true, and less embarrassing than admitting I was this shaken after ten hours in lockup.

She sucked her bottom lip in sympathy. "You got no one to bail you?"

I knew Connor was working to get me out, but the promise was wearing a tad thin. Hunt must be blocking his attempts somehow. "I'm not sure," I said.

I'd been trying to keep my eyes off the clock since it struck seven thirty, but I looked at it now. Two and half hours until Earnest's funeral.

A new officer was on duty this morning. She passed out breakfast to much jeering and griping by my jail mates. On the menu were a plastic bowl of plain grits, (with a plastic spoon, of course), an apple, and a bottle of water. I was starving after skipping dinner last night, so I spooned the first of the lukewarm grits into my mouth with gusto.

My cellmate brought her rations over and sat next to me on my bunk. I shifted over to make room. She sure was friendly.

Abruptly the jagged end of her snapped-off spoon was pressing into my jugular.

Thoughts rushed through my head. The officer was out of sight. I'd miss Earnest's funeral. I'd need my own funeral. My parents would learn I died in prison. Just before Christmas.

"Hand over your breakfast, real nice like, and no one'll get hurt. A skinny bitch like you don't need it."

I passed the apple and grits to her gingerly.

"That's right." The spoon stabbed a little deeper. "And if anyone asks, you weren't hungry."

"Got it," I squeaked. I was too scared to nod.

The spoon left my neck, and she went back over to her bunk.

I sipped my water in an attempt to quiet my gurgling stomach and avoided so much as looking in her direction. There was no note on this one, and it was hard not to give in to my despair. I had no idea how this jail thing worked. All I knew was I wanted out.

"Rough night, huh?" Commander Hunt stood behind the barred door, looking more pleased than I'd ever seen him. Like the cowboy who'd roped the steer only to find out it was his neighbor's prized bull that he'd been coveting for a month.

I pushed myself off the bunk, trying not to grimace at the aching stiffness in my muscles or the picture I must've made with my mascara-streaked cheeks and inevitable zombie hairdo.

"Quite cozy, actually," I said before remembering that pissing him off might not be in my best interest.

His smirk told me he didn't believe me. "Ah well, if you'd like to stay awhile longer, I have some paperwork to do."

I gripped the bars in front of him. "No. Please. I've learned my lesson."

I could see he didn't believe that either.

"I have to be there for Earnest's funeral. For Mrs. Dunst's sake."

His face lost all its humor. "That's the sole reason I'm letting you out right now." He took his time unlocking the cell. "Don't you dare forget it."

"Yes, sir," I said meekly. I felt meek. If he told me that I had to click my heels together three times and wish to go home before he'd let me out, I would've done it without question.

I was not cut out to be a criminal.

I didn't have the balls for it. Or the body for it. I felt every one of my twenty-nine years, and the crick in my neck was so bad I couldn't turn my head. At least it wasn't spouting blood, compliments of my friendly cellmate.

Connor was waiting out front to drive me home. It was just as well. I would've had a great deal of trouble checking my blind spot. He strode up to me and wrapped me in his arms, enveloping me in his clean, fresh scent and calm, competent strength. "I've made sure Hunt won't be pressing any charges, but I'm so sorry I didn't get you out sooner," he murmured.

His concern confirmed my fear that I looked as bad as I expected.

He released me and handed over an espresso and a Danish pastry, which I sorely needed. The pastry was a lot better than the grits I'd almost died for, and the coffee was even more amazing. He opened the car door for me and lapsed into silence, giving me space. I needed that too. I felt drained and shell-shocked and in no way strong enough to face Earnest's funeral.

With LA traffic the way it was, Hunt had barely given me time to shower and change before getting to the church. But the shower was nonnegotiable. Preferably a hot, long one. Maybe I could forgo makeup since I'd probably cry it off anyway, and Earnest had never cared whether I'd worn it.

I'd forgotten Oliver, Etta, Aunt Alice, and Henrietta were coming to the funeral until I walked inside and found them waiting for me.

"Where have you been?"

"Are you okay?"

"Did you spend the night at Connor's again?"

"You better get ready fast; we need to leave in fifteen minutes!"

Without answering any of them, I grabbed a muffin and headed for the shower.

MY NECK, AT LEAST, FELT BETTER after the shower. We headed to the church in two cars. I couldn't bear the idea of being squished in with everyone, so I made the excuse that I might end up staying late or going to Mrs. Dunst's afterward. Oliver took Henrietta and Aunt Alice. Etta came with me. Perhaps sensing the same thing as Connor, she stayed quiet for the drive. LA offered a weak drizzle of rain for the occasion, so we listened to the swoosh of the window wipers and the sounds of traffic.

I was wearing the navy dress I'd worn to my first Taste Society interview, waterproof mascara, and a heavy heart. The dress only fit me thanks to hardly eating yesterday.

I'd known there was a chance we would bury Earnest before we caught his killer. But I hadn't expected us to be back to square one. Even though working on the case had gotten me an overnight stay in jail, I couldn't help but think about it. This time, however, I wouldn't make the mistake of taking action.

If not for the whistle-blowing thing, why would someone want to kill sweet, gentle, do-gooder Earnest? There were so few people who'd had anything to do with him in person over the past three years.

Maybe I could examine everyone's faces during the service and at the cemetery. Didn't killers tend to show up at their victim's funerals? To gloat? Even if that was a myth perpetuated by television dramas, it was a statistical probability that the killer knew Earnest personally, which meant they might have to attend for appearance's sake. Besides, as much as I was sure he'd like to, Hunt couldn't punish me for looking at people.

As we pulled up to the church, I realized that studying everybody's expressions would be easier said than done. The parking lot was already packed to capacity, and cars lined the street. On the one hand, I was glad Mrs. Dunst might see how many lives Earnest had impacted. On the other, the astronomical amount of people who'd shown up meant I'd be lucky to get standing room in the church, let alone be able to search faces.

My group squeezed into the back, unable to avoid brushing against the other mourners. It was stuffy, like Earnest's apartment, but the smell was a dizzying cocktail of perfume, flowers, and body odor rather than stale junk food. I missed the stale junk food scent. And the quiet of just the two of us. Had my funeral group been a few minutes later, we wouldn't have even fit inside the building.

I wanted to find Mrs. Dunst, but it would be difficult to get to her through the crowd and the service was already starting. Beyond cursing Hunt for making me so late, all I could do was hope she had friends by her side.

The minister welcomed us and said a few brief words before handing over the microphone. Jay followed with a beautiful, heartfelt eulogy. He told the story of Earnest's life, painting a vivid picture of the man I'd never had the chance to know, the happy, carefree youth, and finishing with the man he'd become: stronger and purer for having been broken. It had everyone choking up, Jay included. Even Aunt Alice dabbed at a few tears for this man she'd never met.

Judging by my own tissue, my waterproof mascara wasn't living up to its name. All my remaining anger at Jay had melted away with it.

Mrs. Dunst and I had chosen to have a closed casket, reasoning that Earnest would've been uncomfortable with everyone looking at him. So at the end of the service, the few people lucky enough to have gotten seats stood up to sing "The Lord is My Shepherd," and then the coffin bearers carried Earnest down the aisle—to the glorious menace of the *Star Wars* "Imperial March." I found myself laughing and crying at the same time. Earnest would've loved it.

The church emptied rapidly as everyone made their way to the cemetery. I sought out Mrs. Dunst and gave her a hug. "Sorry I couldn't find you earlier."

"It's fine, darling. I'm just glad you're here. And who is this?"

My tagalong group was lingering behind me, so I made introductions, and we walked outside together. Somehow the momentary joy I'd felt was sucked away by the cold wind, leaving me even more fragile than before. We crossed the parking lot and entered the cemetery, the earth soft under our feet from the drizzle. My heels sank into it, and I noticed hundreds of similar holes left by other guests.

As the minister closed with a few final words and the casket was lowered into the ground, I stood beside Mrs. Dunst and held her hand. Although we'd known Earnest was gone for almost a week now, watching the casket disappear below the line of fresh-cut earth brought a sense of painful finality. Her grip was tight in mine.

People made their way toward us to offer condolences. Most of them I didn't recognize. Most of them Mrs. Dunst didn't recognize either, seeing as they were fans of BusiLeaks who had come to show their support. None of them had "murderer" written on their faces.

Dr. Kelly came forward and introduced herself to Mrs. Dunst. She'd swapped her red suit jacket for a black one, and she clasped my hand too. I'd filled Mrs. Dunst in about her and Earnest's secret progress, so there wasn't much to say.

"I'm very sorry to meet you under these tragic circumstances. Earnest was a very strong person, stronger than most, and he learned that from you."

Her expression was serene, of course.

I had my doubts about Kelly, but probably only because she was a shrink.

Mr. Bradley, the landlord, was there too and all of Earnest's neighbors. I was coming back from telling my own support team to go home without me when Humphrey headed my way. His face was strained and his broad shoulders weighed down even more than usual, overly so considering he didn't know Earnest well. Then I noticed the old woman next to him.

She leaned heavily on his arm and smacked him for going too fast and then too slow as they covered the last ten yards. When they stopped, she drew herself up to her full height of five ten, standing awfully steady for someone who'd been leaning so much on Humphrey a moment ago, and sized me up like I was a flasher's shriveled trouser snake.

"Isobel, this is my mother, Mrs. Fierro."

This was the mother he got up at all hours for? I could see the resemblance in their large, heavyset frames and light brown eyes, but I still found it hard to believe. Did she have his one true love locked in her basement or something to keep him obedient?

"So you're the girlfriend," she said. "Next time, organize seating for the seniors. I have a bad knee, and standing in this freezing cemetery makes it worse, you know."

I clenched my jaw to stop it from dropping. *Next time?*

Humphrey's face had grown even more pained. "Sorry." He leaned in and spoke softly. "She goes to a lot of funerals these days, and it's made her . . . blasé."

Mrs. Fierro turned her glower onto him.

"I wanted to offer our condolences," he said, "and also, if you need a hand moving stuff out of the apartment, knock on my door. I'd be happy to help."

"Thank you. That's very kind."

Mrs. Fierro rolled her eyes and then grabbed his arm to be escorted away.

Once again, it put my jail time into perspective. If I had a mother like her, I might have counted it as a relief.

20

AFTER WALKING MRS. DUNST back to her car after the funeral, I went straight home and slept on my wonderfully comfortable bed with Meow for three blissful hours. When I woke up, I decided after days of traumatic events, it was time to switch off from it all and try to restore my inner balance.

For me that meant staying home, baking delicious food, and eating it.

Happily, the apartment was empty of Oliver and guests. I baked a triple batch of chocolate-chip-and-toffee cookies to share between said guests and Mrs. Dunst. Then I made a double batch of gingerbread men for the hell of it since Christmas was just three and a half more days away.

Meow kept me company by stalking cockroaches under the fridge.

She would be my only company on Christmas too. Oliver was flying to England to see his family. Aunt Alice and Henrietta would be leaving soon. Or so I prayed. And Etta had a hot date lined up. If I'd had the money for overpriced Christmas tickets, I would've flown home to spend the holiday with my parents and Lily in a heartbeat. Instead, I'd have to make do with a Skype call.

After plenty of sampling the dough and then the finished product, I bribed myself into exercising by promising to restock my pile of books at the library afterward. I'd drop off the cookies to Mrs. Dunst at the same time.

I exchanged my PJs for sweats, pulled on an old pair of trainers, and knocked on Etta's door.

"I brought cookies," I said.

Her eyes latched onto the plate. "Are you bribing me for something?"

"No. I'm about to go for a walk and thought I'd see if Dudley wanted to come."

Dudley's eyes were latched onto the plate too. It hadn't taken him long to learn that food came in all sorts of shapes and sizes, usually from a person's hand.

"He'd love to. I'll get some bags, treats, and his leash for you."

"Can he go down the stairs now?"

"Oh yes, he's been doing that from day three."

"What?" The day he'd refused to go down the stairs, forcing me to spend time with Aunt Alice and Henrietta, had been day three.

"He's a fast learner," Etta said, mistaking my surprise and handing me all the walking accessories.

I grabbed a cookie as a treat for myself, too, and wondered why Mr. Black had been over yesterday if she didn't need him to carry Dudley. But I wasn't about to ask. I'd done my due diligence and had washed my hands of it. As she'd pointed out, she'd survived on this earth a great deal longer than I had. She could make her own decisions. All the evidence showed they were working out for her, which is more than I could say for mine.

Dudley wanted to do his usual sniff investigation of the stair landing, so I followed him around then hauled him away when he lifted his leg on my dead cactus. I was hoping it would miraculously recover, given no one was supposed to be able to kill a cactus. We headed for the stairs and stopped when Dudley planted his feet at the ledge.

"Oh don't try that again. Etta told me you know how to do them now."

He used his big brown eyes to brainwash me, but I wasn't buying it. I pulled out a treat. "Come on, you can do it." He whined and watched the treat with every fiber of his being, but he didn't step forward. I bit into my cookie while I thought about what to do. His focus shifted to the cookie. Experimenting, I broke off a piece, making sure it was free of chocolate chips, and gave it to him. "Do you like that, boy?"

He liked that.

"Want some more? Come on, take one small step."

He lifted his front leg and waved it over the edge of the stairs before putting it back onto the concrete landing.

I gave him another piece of cookie to reward him for at least trying, then beckoned again.

He repeated the paw wave but still didn't get down to even the first step. "Ugh. You're just like Earnest," I told him sadly. Except I wasn't one of Dudley's special people he trusted enough to overcome his anxieties. I would have to get Etta's help.

With Etta leading the way, Dudley walked carefully down the steps then looked to me for more cookie. Sighing, I handed him another crumb.

I was left with a pathetic pile of chocolate pieces.

Etta laughed at me before returning to her apartment. "Sometimes I think Dudley's better at training humans than the other way around."

"You might be right."

We started walking. The morning drizzle had cleared, and the winter sun was making a halfhearted effort to filter through the clouds. Despite the chill in the air, it was a lovely day. The recent rain had washed away the usual smells of exhaust fumes, dusty asphalt, pot, urine, fast food, and booze and replaced it with that specific, soul-lifting freshness that only long-overdue rain can bring.

Even so, my mind flitted uselessly between the funeral and the case. Like Etta and Mr. Black, both were now out of my hands. I inhaled deeply, determined to put the thoughts aside and enjoy the incredible air and buoyant company.

Dudley waltzed along, practically skipping with excitement every time he caught a new scent or marked a new pole. I wished I could be more like him. Not the peeing on everything part, the simple, joyous part. Humans tend to think we're superior because of our intelligence and use of tools, but who's more content? Animals live in the moment. Dudley might have had a rough past, but he wasn't thinking of it right now. He was enjoying what was in front of him. I was trying to, but I kept dragging Earnest's murder with me.

I blew hair out of my eyes, exasperated with myself, and walked faster. Might as well burn some calories if I couldn't appreciate the day. Along the way, I tried to devise a method of convincing Dudley to walk downstairs with me. What could be more motivating than a cookie? The challenge was similar to coaxing Earnest to leave his home, so I attempted to draw from my experience. Unfortunately, I couldn't see cocaine or psychology working for Dudley.

Two poop bags and forty minutes later, we returned to the apartment building and the dreaded steps. I froze. Dudley stopped and cocked his head at me. All my arm hairs stood to attention. I figured out who might've killed Earnest.

I DROPPED DUDLEY HOME and called Connor to outline my hypothesis. He wasn't as sure as I was but agreed it was plausible. The problem was, we had no proof. Everything was circumstantial. There might be some DNA evidence in the suspect's car or house, but to find it we'd need a warrant. And to get a warrant, we'd need to convince a judge. And to convince a judge, we'd need more than my gut conviction and loosely connecting dots.

Connor told me he'd speak with Hunt and get back to me.

That left me to twiddle my thumbs. Some people can twiddle their thumbs and produce amazing knitting or crocheting works of art. I wasn't one of them, so I went to the library and then Mrs. Dunst's house instead. I came home with an armful of books, four more casseroles (now she knew I had guests to help me eat them), and a burning impatience to hear from Connor.

I started on one of the novels but couldn't concentrate. I fed Meow. I logged into my email and deleted the ones from Aunt Alice in case she ever asked to look. I cleaned out the fridge. I made sure the volume on my phone was up high for the dozenth time. I plucked my eyebrows. I unclenched my jaw. Checked my phone again.

My body still ached from its night in prison, so I ran a hot bath. While I waited for the tub to fill, I discovered an old bottle of "Delicious Bubbles" under the sink, probably left over from a previous tenant, and dumped some of that in too. I'd just stripped down and submerged myself up to my ears when Connor finally called. I sat up and lunged for the phone, sending a wave of bubbles over the side. I wiped more bubbles off my face before answering it. Maybe I'd overdone the Delicious Bubbles.

"We have a plan," he said. "Hunt wasn't happy, but the media have his balls to the wall, and with no better leads, he agreed it was worth checking out."

Connor outlined the details. The LAPD wanted the evening to gather any supporting evidence they could without alerting the suspect, and tomorrow we'd confront the murderer. At least who I hoped was the murderer.

"I can't believe you got Hunt to listen," I said. I'd been sure he'd dismiss the whole thing as soon as Connor mentioned my name. The commander must be very protective of his balls.

An ugly thought occurred to me. Or perhaps I should've said an even uglier thought since the commander's scrotum against a wall was not something I wanted to visualize. He was going to be super mad if he went out on a limb and hit another dead end, especially if the press got wind of it. Would he throw me back in jail if I was wrong?

"I might've told him it was my theory," Connor said. "To make sure he'd give it a fair hearing."

I used my spare hand to fashion a beard of bubbles around my chin. I didn't know whether to be indignant or touched. My beard plopped into the bath. I decided on touched. Connor was trusting me enough to put his own ass on the line.

As if his thoughts had followed the same path, he said, "I hope to hell you're right about this, Avery."

I swiped the remaining bubbles off my chin, suddenly feeling foolish. "I hope so too."

21

I BARELY SLEPT that night. Accrued sleep deprivation made my eyes bleary, but I had too much nervous energy to care. Connor picked me up at eight a.m. because they needed me for the plan to work. He handed me another espresso in a thermos, and I chugged it down, forgetting to enjoy it.

When we arrived at our destination, Hunt was there waiting for us in an unmarked vehicle. He offered me a stiff nod, and I managed to restrain myself from gloating. Just.

I strapped on my wire—a police-issue one this time—and left the boys in the car. At the door, I gave myself a moment to tamp down on my jittery emotions and channel Dr. Kelly's tranquil calm. Time for stage one. I rang the doorbell.

Before I was ready for it, Humphrey was standing in front of me. He was a large, thickset man, but the extra padding around his waist and the slump to his shoulders had stopped me from considering how strong he must be. Until now.

As always, his face was cragged and weather-beaten, like a cliff face slowly being worn down by the relentless beating of the sea. Only in Humphrey's case, the beating came from too many demands and not enough good to counterbalance them.

"Hi, Humphrey. Do you have a few minutes? I brought cookies."

He looked over his shoulder with a harried expression. "Um, well Mother is over, but I guess so." He stepped back, and I followed him down a hallway that was a replica of Earnest's, except without all the posters.

"Would you like a cup of tea?" he asked.

"Please."

"Make me a new cup while you're at it," demanded his mother. "This one's so weak I can hardly taste it."

Humphrey shuffled off to obey, and I sat down with Mrs. Fierro in the small living area. As I'd noted at the funeral, she was tall and big-boned like her son, yet she didn't have his world-weary defeated air. Stuffed into a recliner with a woolen throw over her legs and a walking cane propped by her side, Mrs. Fierro looked ready to fight. Her hair was neatly pinned back, her eyebrows were thin and over-plucked, and her mouth was a slash of painted red. Even the thick, black angular frames of her glasses had attitude.

"Is your knee feeling any better?" I asked her.

"No. That's what old age does. Makes everything worse. My hemorrhoids were dripping with blood this morning. Something for you to look forward to."

"Um. Sorry to hear that." And I was sorry, but I wasn't sure whether it was more for her or myself. "Cookie?"

She snatched one from the plate.

"Must be tough to have a bad knee. Can you walk upstairs with it?" My question was not as casual as it seemed. Nor was it related to Etta's claims. I had no interest in Mrs. Fierro's sex life.

"Pah! You have no idea. I'm confined to flat surfaces like a damn cripple. Next I'll be stuck slithering on my belly like a snake."

Well, she had the right personality for it.

Humphrey saved me from having to formulate an appropriate response by returning with two mugs of tea. I offered him a cookie in gratitude.

"Don't even think about it, Humphrey," said Mrs. Fierro, sending flecks of cookie flying from her mouth. "They're no good for you."

Humphrey put his cookie back.

Holy smokes. How could he bend over backward for this woman and still let her treat him like a three-year-old? Especially when she was such a blatant hypocrite.

The only explanation that made sense was that he'd never gotten far enough away from his mother's shadow to learn perspective. To discover she wasn't always right and that others held different opinions. That he was more valuable and more capable than she'd led him to believe.

And after five minutes with the woman, I was certain she'd never let him. She was a bully through and through.

Unaware of my speculation, Humphrey stared at the cookies wistfully and then turned his shy smile on me. "What can I do for you, Isobel?"

"I was wondering—well, with Earnest gone and eight months of his rental contract remaining—whether you know anyone who could be interested in taking it over?"

He glanced at Mrs. Fierro, who sipped the steaming liquid and puckered her mouth like it tasted rotten. "Well, actually, Mother might want to move in. It would help me respond a lot faster when she needed me for anything. It's hard with the forty-minute drive between us. Worse if traffic is bad."

Mrs. Fierro took another sip and grimaced again. "Pity it won't help you make a damn cup of tea."

Humphrey looked crestfallen, so I took a sip of my own and said, "Mine is lovely, thanks."

Mrs. Fierro shot devil eyes at me. To evade her gaze, I scanned the room. It was clean and neat but furnished bachelor style, with cheap timber veneer furniture, brown fabric couches, and no embellishments or Christmas decorations anywhere. Unlike Earnest's mom, I couldn't imagine Mrs. Fierro would do anything to change that. My eyes were drawn to the sole splash of color. A stack of DVDs on top of the entertainment unit and a packet of Cheetos Bolitas.

Time stopped.

How many US citizens had a thing for Cheetos Bolitas? What were the odds Humphrey did? We'd never recovered the packet Earnest had bought right before he died.

Humphrey and Mrs. Fierro were both staring at me now. I took another sip of tea and tried to remember what we were talking about. "Well, if you're happy to take over the rental contract, that would make things easy," I said. "How soon could you move in?"

"Mother's lease is almost up, so as soon as you wanted, really."

"Great. That sounds convenient for everyone then." I helped myself to a cookie. Mrs. Fierro could rot. "It might need a new paint job once we remove all his posters from the walls. And they have yet to figure out what's going on with the sporadic water pressure or the power outages I'm afraid, so that could take a while for the landlord to fix. I guess you might be able to help them work out what's wrong, Humphrey. You do maintenance stuff for a school, right?"

"Yeah, that's one of my jobs."

I smiled at him and made a show of looking around. "Maybe that's why your apartment is in better condition than Earnest's."

Mrs. Fierro had given up on her tea but appeared disgusted all over again at this information. "I don't want some ramshackle apartment. You can move in there, and I'll have yours."

"I can't move out or my rent would go up, remember, Mother? But I'm sure the landlord would let me paint it for you so you can decorate it however you like."

"Are those Cheetos Bolitas over there?" I interrupted, hoping Connor would get the hint. "They were Earnest's favorite."

Humphrey flinched.

Connor and Hunt rapped hard on the door.

I put my tea down. Time for stage two.

"LAPD. Open up!"

Humphrey's eyes darted around the apartment, looking for an escape route. There was only one way in or out. Without smashing a window anyway.

"Goodness, we better see what's going on," I said, getting up to open the door before they broke it down. Humphrey didn't move to stop me.

Connor and Hunt stormed in, guns in hand, like a pair of badasses in the movies. The plan was to overwhelm. To distract him from the fact our evidence was so scanty. They converged on Humphrey.

"Hands up!" Hunt shouted. "We know you harassed and murdered Earnest for his apartment. You wanted to be close to your aging mother, but with twenty years of rent-controlled pricing, you couldn't afford to move." Humphrey's battered features crumbled. "Your bank records show you're barely scraping by, but your one neighbor with stair-free access was agoraphobic and didn't want to move either. So you tried to force him to."

That was my biggest bit of guesswork. I'd been asking myself for days why anyone would want to kill sweet, gentle Earnest if it wasn't for his whistle-blowing. So when I'd found myself annoyed by sweet, gentle Dudley's refusal to go down the stairs, it had planted a seed in the back of my mind.

But who would Earnest's agoraphobia inconvenience aside from the people who loved him most? He was a good tenant who paid his rent on time despite all the maintenance issues they'd been having. That made me think of Mr. Bradley complaining about all the long-term tenants who wouldn't move out of his rent-controlled apartments. If none of them wanted to move out, what happened if someone wanted to move in?

Humphrey was shaking his head, but there was little conviction behind it, like he'd already given up. His outstretched hands were shaking too.

"We know your apartments share a crawl space where you left dead animals under Earnest's floor to stink the place out," Hunt continued. "We found your prints down there as well as on the hot water pressure valve and the fuse box, which are both mysteriously malfunctioning despite the efforts of numerous plumbers and electricians. But it wasn't enough, was it? Earnest wouldn't leave no matter what you did to his apartment. So you had to escalate things."

Hunt paused for breath.

Humphrey's gaze had fallen to the floor, perhaps wishing he was back in the cramped, dark safety of that crawl space. His hands were still raised, and every now and then, his head gave the slightest half shake of denial.

After I'd put the first puzzle pieces together, Humphrey's kind offer to help me move Earnest's stuff out, despite the burden he was already shouldering with two jobs and his mother, seemed suspicious. It would certainly make life easier if she lived next door. But he was quiet and shy, and I couldn't see him plotting murder, so I'd dismissed him and gone back to pondering how to motivate Dudley to go down the stairs without Etta.

Since cookies and praise hadn't worked, I wondered if the negative motivation of Meow stalking after him might. Had Humphrey's thoughts taken the same turn? That he might be able to persuade Earnest to leave if enough bad things happened in the apartment? There had been an awful lot of maintenance issues that confounded the tradesmen called out to fix them. And I thought Humphrey had once mentioned being a facilities and maintenance worker for a local school. So he'd have the skills for it.

Except none of his efforts had worked. If it were for his own sake, he would've surely given up, but he had his bully of a mother to please.

"Will we find Earnest's prints on that bag of Cheetos?" Hunt asked Humphrey now. He looked better after pausing for breath. Whereas Humphrey looked much worse. His face had gone an unhealthy shade of white, making the voluminous dark pouches under his eyes stand out in severe contrast. "And when we search your car, what are our chances of finding Earnest's DNA in it? You had to transport him to the abandoned building in Exposition Park somehow, didn't you?"

That was the crux of this whole case. And Hunt was bluffing. This entire setup was designed to gather sufficient "probable cause" to convince a judge to issue a search warrant for Mr. Fierro's car and home. Without that DNA, my theory was flimsy enough to collapse under Humphrey's first shy smile at the jury.

"Your own testimony places you in the ideal position to follow Earnest the night of his murder, where in cold blood, you forced the needle into his arm. Maybe you hadn't thought about how much he'd fight, so to cover for the bruising, you took his wallet and phone so it would look like he'd been mugged. Then you drove to one of his old drug hangouts and dumped his body with the syringe next to him to make it seem like he'd overdosed." Hunt paused again. "That's cold, Mr. Fierro. I'm placing you under arrest for the premeditated murder of Earnest Dunst. You have the right to remain—"

"No!" Humphrey pleaded, his gaze snapping up from the floor. "I was only trying to get him evicted."

"—silent. Anything you say can and will be held against you—"

Humphrey was shaking his head vigorously. "You don't understand. I only wanted him to break the terms of his lease by using heroin again. He wasn't supposed to die!"

"Shut up, Humphrey." Mrs. Fierro rose to her feet, her face furious. "Can't you see you just confessed? You useless, worthless, sniveling excuse for a son! You couldn't even do this one thing for me without screwing it up. Who's going to look after me while you're rotting in prison, huh?" She picked up her mug of cooling tea and threw it at him, drenching both Humphrey and Hunt.

"Cuff her too, Stiles. For assaulting a police officer." Connor moved to obey, but he underestimated the snake. She whipped out her walking cane and cracked him straight in the nose.

Blood streamed onto his immaculate white shirt.

Tea dripped from Hunt's mustache.

Connor wrenched the cane from Mrs. Fierro and cuffed her.

I dug through my handbag and handed him the washed handkerchief I'd been meaning to give back. Then I looked over the disastrous scene again. "Well," I said. "I guess we have enough for a warrant now."

CONNOR'S NOSE WAS STILL BLEEDING by the time Hunt had loaded the Fierros into his car and driven off.

"Should I call Levi?" I asked. "I have his direct number."

"Don't even think about it." The effect of Connor's glare was impeded by the handkerchief pressed to his face.

"But what if it's broken? We can't risk ruining your perfection."

"The answer's still no. But it's good to hear you think I'm perfect." His normally rich voice was made nasally by the pressure he was applying to his nose.

"Well, I did. Until you got beat up by an old lady."

His glower made my knees tremble, even with the handkerchief this time. "She caught me off guard. Besides, you think Etta couldn't take you out?"

Touché.

"Sure she could. That's why I make sure to be nice to her."

"By that logic, why aren't you nice to me?"

I gave him my sweetest smile. "Because I know you won't take me out. It'd be a waste after all the effort you've put into saving my ass."

He removed the handkerchief. "If you're not in the car by the time my key's in the ignition, I'm leaving you here."

Another drop of blood leaked from one nostril.

"Are you sure you don't want me to drive?"

He strode to the SUV and produced a fresh handkerchief. "Not a chance."

We pulled away from Earnest's apartment. Maybe for the last time. Mrs. Dunst had told me she'd let Jay take what equipment he wanted and use a smidgen of the money Earnest left her to pay professional movers to put the rest in storage. Until she could face looking through it one day.

I stared at the old white brick building until it disappeared from view. I'd spent two and a half happy months in those walls. Possibly the happiest two and a half months of my life since the divorce. But it wasn't the walls that I'd miss.

I'd had enough of crying lately, so I focused on the good stuff. We'd caught Earnest's murderer. That was good. But I'd already pitied Humphrey for having Mrs. Fierro as a mother, and now I pitied him even more.

His claim that he'd only intended to get Earnest kicked out for using heroin rang true. It fit with everything I'd observed about him, rather than that he was a cold-blooded killer. And it would be easy enough for the inexperienced to mix up a dose.

Oh yeah, I was supposed to be focusing on the good.

The one silver lining I could see was that at least in prison Humphrey would be free from the reign of terror of his mother. And maybe on a manslaughter rather than homicide charge, he'd get out just after the witch passed away.

Maybe.

I promised myself I'd call my own amazing mother when I got home.

The other problem weighing me down was that we'd failed to achieve the other half of the justice Earnest would've wanted.

The sociopaths over at Aptech were up to something. Something big enough to bribe Jay with a cool hundred grand cash and chop up a cadaver for threat material. Something big enough that Earnest had hired me.

I couldn't let them get away with it.

But with the hard drives erased and the flash drive missing, what else could I do?

22

AUNT ALICE DIDN'T seem quite so bad after getting to know Mrs. Fierro, but I still wanted her and Henrietta out of LA. Preferably with a Pacific Ocean between us.

Unfortunately for me, after almost a week spending every spare second in each other's company, Oliver and Henrietta were smitten with each other. I had a feeling that meant not only would I have to put up with Henrietta, but that Aunt Alice would visit LA a whole lot more often too.

Meow and Dudley, for their part, were learning to tolerate each other from opposite sides of the room, which put them well ahead of me and the lovebirds. We were supposed to be having a movie night, but it had morphed into a make-out session while I'd gone to get popcorn, and I couldn't bring myself to go back. Even Meow had moved to the other couch. I could hardly stand to be in the apartment.

I sat down on Dudley's nest in the kitchen and fed him some of the popcorn. I was looking after him again because Etta had a gentleman friend over, and I guess she didn't want to be interrupted. Since Dudley had taken to being within six feet from her at all times, I could see how it might cramp her style.

"This is what it comes down to, hey boy? We've both been booted out of our own homes because our living companions are getting their game on." We shared some more popcorn. "Why don't we ditch this joint and go to my bedroom?"

The movie was almost finished now anyway. First though, I'd have to clear enough room on my bedroom floor for his gigantic bed. I kissed him on the nose and gave him a few more pieces of popcorn to keep him going. "I'll be right back."

I was hanging up the last piece of clothing when I heard shouting. Heart accelerating, I dove for my bag, grabbed the trusty Taser, and quietly turned the door handle. Someone screamed. A rush of adrenaline jolted through me, but I forced myself to edge the door open slowly, hoping to gain the advantage of surprise. Another door slammed, and Oliver burst out laughing.

Thoroughly confused, I raced into the open living area and found Meow and Dudley tentatively sniffing noses. Meow's fur was lying flat, and Dudley was only trembling a little bit. Henrietta was nowhere to be seen.

"What in the world just happened?" I asked, rushing over to Dudley and Meow in case I needed to intervene. To my surprise, Meow began rubbing herself against Dudley's legs. Dudley looked as shocked and confused as I was but otherwise okay.

Oliver finished laughing and sat down with a big sigh. "Henrietta and I broke things off."

"What? Why?"

"Well, the movie ended and we were talking about places we'd like to travel to, and she said, ugh, you should have heard her." His voice took on a high, whiny pitch as he imitated Henrietta. "Oh, Olly. I can't wait for you to take me around London. I've always wanted to meet the Queen." He shook his head in disgust. "Can you imagine? I can't believe I let things get so far with a bloody Queen fanatic. From Australia no less. I mean, that's almost *more* offensive than my fellow Englishmen loving the monarchy. All hail the Queen who sent the convicts she didn't want to our great land and still pretends to rule it today. I don't understand some people!"

"Um." I bit my lip to keep from laughing. "Sorry to hear. But what happened? I heard shouting and a scream, and now Dudley and Meow have decided to be friends?"

He flopped a lazy hand at them. "Ah well, Meow never liked Aunt Alice *or* Henrietta if I was honest with myself. When I told Henrietta it wasn't going to work out, she lost all that composure I admired her for and started shouting at me. Meow got a fright and took off to find cover, and Dudley came over to investigate what all the noise was about and happened to slip his wet nose right up Henrietta's skirt. That was the shriek you would've heard. Then she stormed out, and Meow decided Dudley might not be such a bad chap after all."

I hid my smile in Dudley's soft fur and scratched Meow in her favorite spot under her chin. I had a feeling Aunt Alice and Henrietta wouldn't stick around LA much longer.

DUDLEY'S ACCIDENTAL COURAGE the night before helped me walk into the 27th Street Community Police Station with a straight spine. Hunt wanted to talk to me. Somehow I doubted it was to apologize.

It was another overcast day, making the gray bricks of the station look even more dreary than normal. I'd showered and eaten a huge breakfast before coming, just in case I was about to be thrown in jail again.

Police Commander Hunt sat me down at his desk this time instead of the interrogation room. A promising sign. The coolness in his blue eyes was less promising. I scanned his belongings for any clues about his personal life. There weren't any. That included a distinct lack of family photos. Etta would be delighted.

"I called you in here as a courtesy. To give you an update." He spat the words out like they tasted bad. "Judge Wong issued a warrant, and we found the DNA evidence we expected in Mr. Fierro's car as well as some on his clothes and those Cheetos. Mr. Fierro confessed everything. Except for anything that might incriminate his mother, that is. She's keeping her mouth shut, but we've charged her with assault, so she'll serve a few months' time. Mr. Fierro will be tried with manslaughter. He told us where he stashed the phone and wallet too. Buried them in the garden and planted seedlings on top. No bloody wonder nothing turned up in our search of the dumpsters around the drug den."

Huh. The seedlings I'd watched him plant. Maybe I wouldn't confess that detail to anyone.

"The flash drive Ms. McCarthy was so eager to get her hands on was in the wallet, undamaged. It contains the plans for an illicit backdoor in the Pearl smartphone operating system Aptech was developing, which would've allowed them to collect all the personal data of the phone users. If the Pearl phones were popular, they could've sold it for millions, if not billions, to the highest bidder. Coleman and McCarthy have been arrested on conspiracy, and there'll be more arrests to come."

In the words of Mrs. Dunst: sweet cartwheeling weasels! The possibilities for evil would've been endless. Emptying bank accounts. Identity theft. Money laundering. Selling personal photos, emails, and documents of high-profile figures to competitors or the press. Big brother government. Aiding terrorist activities with information and building access.

Earnest was a hero.

Not that it was news to me, but perhaps I'd return some of those reporters' calls so the rest of the world could hear about it.

I realized I was smiling.

Hunt was not. "Don't let this success go to your head, Avery. Civilians should stay out of police business. As should the Taste Society." He stood up. My cue to go. "I hope I don't see you again. Feel free to leave town."

I stood up too. The words "Yes, Commander" were on my lips, and half my mind was already walking out meekly, but something held me in place. Connor had told me not to be afraid of Hunt, and I knew he wasn't, but my fear was not a thing I could switch off. Earnest, though, he had been afraid. Of leaving his home. Of relapsing. Of being targeted for being brave enough to speak up. But he hadn't let it stop him.

I was going to take a leaf out of Earnest's book.

"I'd like to say it's been a pleasure, Commander, but it really hasn't." I picked up a pencil from his tidy desk and tapped it against his chest. "Maybe you should get your facts straight before blustering on about civilians staying out of police business. It was me who solved your case. Connor just told you it was his idea so you'd listen." Ignoring the mottled crimson coloring his neck, I slipped the pencil into his breast pocket and gave it a pat. "So next time the media has your balls to the wall, don't come to me."

23

TO CELEBRATE the wrapping up of both the Aptech and Earnest cases, I made myself a cup of tea, grabbed a gingerbread-man cookie and a book, and got comfortable on Etta's outdoor sofa. If Oliver and I had to squeeze past the darn thing every time we crossed the stair landing we shared with Etta, we might as well take her up on the offer to use it.

The sun had surfaced from behind the clouds, and while the air was no longer fresh from the rain, it was somewhat comforting to return to the mishmash of human scents that said life would go on in Los Angeles.

Even my cactus looked a tad greener. Maybe all it had needed was some watering. Or Dudley's pee.

The loss of Earnest still hurt, and I wasn't ready to consider what my next client might be like, so I opened up the book and lost myself in its pages. This one was a romance. I'd had my fill of murder mysteries for a while.

A shift in the sofa cushion brought me back to reality. Connor was sitting beside me. His heavily bruised nose bore mute witness to the fact he wasn't a cyborg, but even so, he took my breath away. He was handsome enough to be the leading man in any romance. And for some reason, he was here with me.

I reminded myself that I'd managed to drop three pounds in the stress of the past few days and wasn't looking too bad either. I'd brushed my hair today and only had six more pounds to lose. Seven if I had another cookie.

He handed me a thermos and the unmistakable bold, caramel aroma of espresso drifted up from it. "I heard Hunt gave you the good news," he said.

"Yeah, he did." My mind flashed back to my final words to him, and I suddenly wished I had a blanket to pull around me. But it was all right, I reassured myself, Los Angeles was a big enough town that I shouldn't have to ever see the commander again.

I put the cold dregs of my tea down and took a sip of espresso. "CNN is doing a feature story on Earnest, and they'll be interviewing Mrs. Dunst and Jay and me this afternoon. I think it will be good. For Mrs. Dunst and Jay, I mean. Not that it'll make their loss any less . . ."

"What about you?" Connor asked. "How are you holding up?"

I swished espresso on my tongue, letting its rich, dark comfort wash over me. "I'm okay. Or at least I will be okay."

We sat in companionable silence for a while, enjoying the meager sunshine and the lack of anything urgent to do.

"You might be wondering why I'm here," Connor said.

I had been wondering, but I didn't want to drive him away by asking.

The silence stretched out again, except for the sounds of traffic and the faint shouting of my downstairs neighbors, the Flanagans. No doubt they'd be having make-up sex soon. As Etta put it, they were always fighting or fornicating.

Connor shifted beside me. "I'm here because . . . Well, I'd prefer not to go another three months without seeing you."

My head whipped around to see if he was teasing.

He loosed a breath and met my eyes. "Isobel. Izzy. You're the most impossible woman I've ever met. You're hardheaded and stubborn, to the point of foolishness at times. You have an unhealthy addiction to coffee and cookies, wouldn't know fashion if it lived next door, and are so busy looking for the good in people that you have an unfortunate tendency to chat up the bad guys. And I admire you for it. Your warm, genuine, gung-ho nature is so refreshing in this city where superficial style and success is obsessed over beyond all reason, to the degree that it leads to selfishness, deceit, backstabbing, and murder."

"Could have something to do with your line of work," I observed helpfully.

"Would you shut up and let me finish? This is hard for me."

I shut up.

"The point is. I'd like to see you more often. When work permits. Would you like to come to Christmas with my family on Sunday?"

FROM THE AUTHOR

I hope you enjoyed THE HUNGER PAINS. That way I can rub it in my brother's smug face since he scoffed at me when I first started writing at the tender age of sixteen. If you want to help me make sure he gets his comeuppance, take a minute to leave me a review, tell a friend, or tell lots of friends on social media. That'll show him.

As a small token of my appreciation for everyone who already did this for EAT, PRAY, DIE, I drew you this picture of my brother eating humble pie. Enjoy!

My brother eating humble pie

Hungering for more?

SEE ALL THE BOOKS IN THE SERIES AT

CHELSEAFIELDAUTHOR.COM

ACKNOWLEDGEMENTS

Thanks go to my underpaid but much appreciated beta readers: James, Tess, John, Rosie, Bec, Mel, and Mum (because, of course, mothers are the most objective people in the world). I couldn't have done it without you.

To the proofreaders and final pass editors at Victory Editing, thank you for pointing out my every mistake. It's nice to feel inadequate. Oh, and to feel confident my readers won't be pulled out of the story by stray typos or superfluous commas.

Speaking of my inadequacies, thanks to both God and my husband, for loving me anyway. Even when I eat all the chocolate and won't get out of bed except for more chocolate.

Made in the USA
Coppell, TX
01 May 2025